D0744651

The HOUR *of*
BAD DECISIONS

The HOUR of BAD DECISIONS

Russell WANGERSKY

Edited by Edna Alford.
Book and cover design by Duncan Campbell.
Cover image, "Man Walks Towards Town" by Kamil Vojnar / Getty Images.

Printed and bound in Canada at Marquis Book Printing Inc.

Library and Archives Canada Cataloguing in Publication

Wangersky, Russell, 1962–
The hour of bad decisions / Russell Wangersky.

ISBN 1-55050-337-5

I. Title.

PS8645.A5333H52 2006   C813'.6   C2006-901076-5

2   3   4   5   6   7   8   9   10

2517 Victoria Ave.
Regina, Saskatchewan
Canada   S4P 0T2

AVAILABLE IN CANADA & THE US FROM
Fitzhenry & Whiteside
195 Allstate Parkway
Markham, ON, Canada, L3R 4T8

The publisher gratefully acknowledges the financial assistance of the Saskatchewan Arts Board, the Canada Council for the Arts, the Government of Canada through the Book Publishing Industry Development Program (BPIDP), Association for the Export of Canadian Books, and the City of Regina Arts Commission, for its publishing program.

CONTENTS

Burning Foley's

FOLEY'S HOUSE WAS BURNING.

You could see it from the top of the hill, from on top of the long green slope that led down into Cuslett.

There was old meadow on one side of the narrow, crumbling highway, matted spruce on the other. And in the meadow, which ran down in a rush to the river, individual and perfectly conical spruce trees coming up, dark blue-green and full, their skirts right down into the long grass, keeping the wind out. In the town, there were a handful of houses, a blocky red barn, and the long, curving river twisting down to Placentia Bay. It was the kind of small place dwarfed by its surroundings, the swooping spruce hills on both sides of the valley, the huge summer sky rising up over the vast silver bay.

A slight heat-shimmer in the air, the day just warm enough that the air over the road had a gentle tremble, so that the corners and roof-lines of the houses wavered ever so slightly.

Other than that, there was no motion at all, no cars on the road, and from the distance of the top of the hill, no sounds either, as if Cuslett were holding its breath, waiting for someone familiar to arrive and wake the place.

Except for James Foley's house. Burning.

Roy Meade could see it, could smell the smoke and the gasoline on the cuffs of his work shirt. And he sat high on the hillside, watching, his brother, Tony, sitting just a few feet away. Roy was singing tunelessly under his breath, his mouth slightly open.

"I don't know," Tony said. He was fiddling with a long piece of meadow grass.

"Shut up, Tony. Jest shut up."

An inverted cone of black and dirty yellow smoke, rising and roiling straight up in the still air. The smoke was pillowing into itself, with the rounded bulges being caught from beneath by the next, faster-rising, still hotter breath from the fire below. Already, there was the distinct and tangled smell of the smoke in the air, that curious, almost dump-fire smell of someone's possessions burning. Around the burning building, inconsequential figures were running back and forth. Then the roof tar was well alight, with its particular orange flame and the heavy, even-blacker smoke, the roof buckling in the middle, edges shrugging up, the centre falling in with a whoosh of reaching smoke and flame, sparks and flankers showering down on the running figures. And then the too-late fire trucks pounding down the highway, red lights on and sirens screaming, air brakes smoking heavily from the long, winding trip along the shore from Placentia.

Foley's house was the green one – or it had been green. It used to have windows, too, but the frames had burned, and the windows were gone, toppling either back into the flames or outwards to lie face-down in the grass. One window had blown out early, when the fire was hottest, scattered the grass with long, sharp knives of soot-blackened glass. The clap-board was smoking and falling off the outside of the house in sheets as the nails lost their grip on the sheathing, the dry wood popping and crackling angrily as the flames roared over it.

And Foley's was far from being the first house to burn in Cuslett.

The welfare house by the beach had burned, too, a few weeks earlier, the family off in Placentia on a grocery trip. It was an old two-storey, three-bedroom, hard to heat, down on the flats where Roy Meade had his wood piled, the rising heaps of sharp-pointed posts and the eight-foot, thin longers. The family had lived there for three weeks. Meade hadn't even waved hello.

That time, the fire department arrived in time to soak down the charred main beams; the walls had fallen in before the trucks got there. After the fire, the only things left were the chimney and the Enterprise oil stove, squatting down heavily where the kitchen had been. The stove still intact, its white glazing all crazy-cracked from the heat, the cracks milky from smoke. The trees on what had been the back of the house had their leaves seared black on the side nearest to the fire. The RCMP parked in the driveway overnight, as if something might change in the misting ruin, as if somehow someone might tamper with the steaming beach fire remnants. It smelt like a beach fire, too, the kind of fire that had been doused with salt water and left behind after everyone piled into the car and headed back to town.

Eventually, the police headed back to town, too, unable to find the cause.

The fall before, two summer cabins burned on the same weekend that their owners had packed up and gone home, the cabins well up on the river flats behind the town where the Meades had their sheep pasture, fences running for straight-edged miles through the alder scrub and the small rectangles of clearcut. Roy Meade suggested it might have been a chimney fire in the smaller cabin nearest the river, because he had never liked the look of the angled and rusting stovepipe, and he knew they burned green wood anyway. Meade said he had seen the fires while he was well back on the flats where the river first came down from the barrens.

The post office burned, and the house the police used when the roads drifted in.

And Mercy Lang's house burned in the snow while the Langs were snowbound in St. Brides during a storm. And then the abandoned house under the cliff edge, which burned late at night, so bright in the January dark that the red-rock cliff was lit from bottom to top, thirty feet or more, like an overdrawn backdrop to a small and burning one-act play.

The road in to the abandoned house was long grown over and filled in two feet deep with snow, so the fire trucks didn't try to get in to put out the fire, and the firefighters stood next to their grumbling trucks instead and watched the huge fire throw its shadows onto the cliff. And in the morning, when the sun came up bright and winter-hard, the snow was melted and yellow six or eight feet from the foundation, and a great yellow and brown wedge of dirty snow extended away from the foundation in the direction the wind had been blowing, the snow stained by the falling embers and ash. By the time the police arrived, all of Cuslett had been to see the ruins, and hundreds of footprints twined and spun through the snow like wild strawberry runners, and no one could tell which ones might have been the very first footprints in.

The police didn't stay for that one, just looked at the twisting footprints, got back into the cars and drove away.

The police stayed longer at Foley's: while the foundation was still smoking, they surrounded the property with police tape. They found Foley inside, in a corner of the kitchen. The coroner said later Foley had died from the smoke, although you couldn't tell from the blackened body they brought out of the charcoal, his arms and legs pulled up tight to his body where the heat had shrunk all his sinews. It looked too small to be Foley, but it was. Plenty of policemen

then, most in white overalls sifting through the blackened bits and charcoal and remains with shovels; finding a belt buckle and the batteries from a flashlight,
coils of copper wire with the insulation all burned
away, the welded workings of an ancient pocket
watch. Finding every single bit that couldn't burn:
finding nothing else.

Roy Meade was stripping and piling spruce fence
posts near the beach by that afternoon, the air sharp
with the smell of sap. Meade's hands were black and
tacky with the sticky resin, and the axe handle had
distinct palm and fingerprints all along the length of
its varnished wood. He was standing behind the big
berm of beach rocks thrown up by the swells,
between the rocks and the long, brown, peaty curl of
the river, and he was using the axe to chip long, thick
points onto one end of each post. It was wild river
meadow there, isolated clumps of blue flag iris, nodding heads of Queen Anne's lace, and the fresh new
grass still supple and not yet beginning to yellow.
Damselflies working low over the water's surface,
turning and wheeling and fluttering high, their crys-
talline wings catching the light as they rose from the
water in mating flight.

The river slow there – it comes in fast, dropping
out of the hills and light-brown from draining the
great, peat-bound barrens, but it loses all its speed as
it swings against the back of the barrier beach,
becoming deep and steady, taking its time to reach
the near end of the beach where a gap in the stones
let the river bleed brown into the sea.

Meade worked steadily, the thunk of his axe rever-
berating across the flat of the valley bottom, only
occasionally silent when he stopped to stack more
finished posts on the pile. All the posts the same
length, piled evenly, the rough bark and its long-
fingered, fine lichen torn by handling. Meade smelled
like sweat and two-stroke engine oil. He wore a dirty
black baseball cap, "CAT" written on the front, jammed
down on his head, and his movements were spare and
mechanical, the shortest possible distance between
points. He watched someone walking along the short
beach road towards him, skirting the muddy puddles
from the heavy rain that had fallen overnight. The sky
was blue now, the deep, reaching blue of late June, the
heat already shrinking the puddles.

Tony Meade looked at his brother using the axe to
trim the last few straggling branches from the posts,
the small feathery branches the chain saw always
missed, then turning each post towards the ground to
make the points, sharp strokes with the axe, the white,
long chips flying. Chips were lying all around, some
new, some older and starting to yellow as the wood
weathered. The wind full in off the bay, the air briny.
A few chips had flown far enough to lie in the stead-
ies at the edge of the river, and they floated, turning
gently, surrounded by the small iridescent pools of oil
that leached quickly from the sap-bleeding bark.

"Never the idea," Tony said. He was a big man,
almost six feet tall, but not as big as his brother, and
he had his thumbs hooked in the front pockets of his
jeans, his fingers tapping his legs nervously while he

talked. Tony's face was thin, his lips pursed as if he were tasting something slightly bitter.

"Wha?" Roy looked up from chopping, his dark face blank, straightening up and pulling his shoulders back, stretching. Roy was big but spare, with the wiriness of constant motion. Except in his face: his usual expression was still and almost expressionless, even his slight smile not without a hint of menace.

"Never the idea to burn no one," Tony said. "Never th' idea at all."

"His fault." Roy shrugged. "Weren't supposed to be home. That were your job. You said he wunn't be home."

Roy stopped and leaned the axe against the back wheel of his pickup truck. The box on the back of the truck had rusted away, replaced by a flatbed of two-by-six boards, nailed flat, with stakes on the sides to hold the load in. The sides of the truck were spattered with mud, and a case of beer, one flap open, sat in the back. Roy Meade reached in, took a beer, twisted the top off and dropped the cap back into the box. He stared at his brother for a moment before speaking.

"You said Thursday nights he's in St. Brides. Not s'posed to come back."

"Still..." Tony said.

"No car in th' shed. Couldn't know." Either way, Roy didn't look particularly upset. He drank a quick swallow of beer, and scratched the back of his neck. Across the flats, a group of crows were flying loosely, fighting over something one crow was carrying in its mouth. The others put up a raucous cawing, tumbling in the air.

James Foley's wake was in St. Bride's, at his sister's house. The family held it as soon as the coroner released the body, while the police were still talking homicide and "no suspects" and "investigation continuing." The family set up the casket in the living room. That day, a Wednesday, the room filled quickly, Foleys up from Barachoix and Placentia, one or two from Branch and a nephew, an oil rigger, all the way from Alberta. Foley's sister crying quietly in her hands, the noise muffled by her fingers, the other Foleys and some friends talking softly.

Around two o'clock, there was a sound at the door, and Roy Meade came in, and the room was suddenly silent.

Meade walked over to the closed casket under the front window. He looked around the room at the silent and watching Foleys.

"Shame," Meade said. He examined his hands, turning them over, tore a loose scrap of skin off from next to his thumbnail. There was a ring in his dark hair from the hat, which was pushed into the back pocket of his jeans. No one else spoke.

It was a small, fussy room, overfilled with photographs, the flat surfaces topped with runners. A ship's clock on the mantel, and a faint scent of must; a coal grate, unlit, centered in the side wall, and all around, a crowd of soft, faded furniture. Meade looked steadily around the room, a moment for each person, as if he were taking count. Then he turned around and left, a faint hint of pitch lingering in the air behind him.

The Foleys heard his truck start in the yard and pull away, and still the room was quiet, except for the steady step of the clock.

There was one pool table in the lounge in St. Bride's, but it sat crooked on the slanted floor, and only strangers ever tried to actually play on it. Roy sat as far away from the pool table as was possible, on the last seat near the wall where you could look up and watch the bright afternoon light shine in through the dirty glass and the wire grating that covered the outside of the windows.

When he had come in, his eyes had been dazzled by the bright sunlight outside, and he had thought the bar was empty. But after he ordered a beer and his eyes began to adjust to the light, he saw three men stand up from behind the pool table, pushing their chairs back, the scrape of the legs loud in the empty room.

The three men, all Langs, walked up to him at the bar; Mercy's son and two of her nephews. They stood in close to Roy. He watched the condensation form and then quickly pool around the base of his beer glass. The room smelled of old beer and disinfectant. Meade could smell the Langs.

"Whatcha going ta do? Burn us out, too?" Kevin Lang, the son. All three laughed, and it was an unpleasant sound.

The three of them had been cut from the same cloth, all three dark, blocky and threatening. Almost shoulder to shoulder with each other, standing over him as he sat at the bar. Roy drank his beer.

"So I laughed, too," Meade told Tony later that night, imitating himself gruffly – "haha, haha," flat and wooden like a crow croaking.

Even later, the moon came up full and yellow over the too-black hills. By one o'clock, it was falling again, and by three, clouds rolled across and the night was suddenly dark.

It was cool, the air rich with the complicated smells of summer. The wet of the dew, the fine wick of the juniper rolling down from the barrens. Rhodera, leaves waxy and smooth, its complex resin almost reminiscent of eucalyptus, exhaling softly into the night. Damp moss and blueberry, ground cranberry and mash berry, each one adding a new and particular note.

In one corner of the meadow, the sheep moved by instinct, pushing up against each other, tight enough for the branch ends on the longers – the long fence slats – to pull tufts from the wool of the sheep pressed against the fence.

Roy Meade moved across the meadow carrying a stick, the tip of a spruce tree, branches cut away. The stick was about ten feet long, the end wrapped tightly in rags. Meade was carrying a red plastic gas can, too, and he walked up a short hill directly behind the Lang's house before opening the can and pouring gas over the rags.

He carefully screwed the cap back on before taking out his lighter. He flicked it and then touched the flame to the rags. For a moment, he stared straight at the torch, watching the soot yellow flames at the edges, the blues in close to the cloth, turning the flaring torch slowly.

There were a lot of other things Roy might have seen, if he had been looking.

He might have seen the flames dripping from the end of the torch, yellow drops making fluttering, zipping sounds as they fell, and walking towards the back of the house, he might have seen the small burning islands the fallen drops left on the dark sea of the ground, flaring brilliant and burning themselves out. He might have seen how black the yellow gas flames made the rest of the night, how they licked and curled liquid up from the rags, might have seen how the flames stood out like a signal.

He might have imagined the three Langs sleeping by then in their small upstairs rooms, imagined their heavy snoring or the twitching, shallow moments of their dreams. Imagined that cold, first waking moment of fear when the room lit up in flickered orange, the tin taste of fear and the sinking ceiling of heavy smoke inching down the walls.

But he saw none of it, and imagined nothing. Meade simply held the torch up against the eaves, right where the electrical service came into the building, watching as the flames took hold and licked quickly over the roof. Reaching as far as he could, he used the edge of the roof to scrape the still-burning cloth from the spruce pole, and then walked down into the meadow to bury the wood in amongst its fellows.

The tar on the roof burned greedily, the light of it casting great, long, staggering shadows and quickly colouring the meadow orange. Without looking back, Meade walked away.

The next morning, Roy Meade walked into the senior's home in St. Bride's, holding the papers in one hand, the liquor store bag in the other. Two bottles of Schenley's Golden Wedding rattled against each other in the bag, the neck of the paper twisted over and over again so that the light brown kraft paper had permanent, soft-spiraled wrinkles.

Meade unwound the top of the bag as he walked into a bright room where an elderly man lay strapped in tight under white sheets, his arms free, a tray with half the morning's breakfast still sitting there, and a pair of glasses. Meade moved the tray, put the papers on the table and swung it across in front of the man.

"This is where you sign," he said.

"Is this land near Foley's?" the man said, squinting. Meade open the drawer next to the man's bed, slid one of the two bottles in on its side, and watched the bubbles race up the inside of the label.

"Yeah," he said. "Near Foley's. You remember."

The land registry in Placentia had burned decades before, leaving many pieces of land as the preserve of memory and good fences. Affidavits were to prove clear title, affidavits from men and women old enough to remember whose father had owned which land, and what abutted what. Meade held the first affidavit flat for the man.

"You sign there," he repeated. "I'll witness."

"Can't get the rights of it," the man in the bed said. "Hectares and metres an' all. Says here off the side of the road and down next to the river. Bottom land's always belonged to Foleys. Sure you got it right?"

"Sure am. Like always," Meade said smoothly. "It's always been Meades," he said, pulling the document back as soon as the signature was on it. "Bottle's in the drawer."

Then the same thing next door, two affidavits, and Meade walked slowly down the polished floor towards his truck, rolling the newly-signed papers in his pitch-stained hands.

Two weeks later, the heat had come in full in the valley, and the air was full of stouts, the angry, biting flies with their zigzag rainbow eyes. The new sheep in the meadow weren't used to the windless valley, having spent more time in the windswept community pasture on the barrentops, where the flies were kept at bay by the cold and steady wind from the water. The flies bit the anxious new sheep around their eyes, so they bled bloody, steady tears, butting blindly with each other and trying to force themselves deeper into the flock to escape the biting clouds.

Nearby, Roy Meade's truck was heavy-laden, piled high with new fenceposts. He was standing next to the truck, pounding a post into the ground with a log maul, sweat showing at the armpits of his shirt and in a T across his back. A straight line of similar posts stretched away to the trees, longers lying in the grass and not yet nailed on.

A car stopped on the road, and its driver leaned out the window and called out to Roy.

"That's Foley's meadow."

Roy stopped pounding the stake into the ground.

"Not the way I remember it." And he stared until the driver put the car in gear and drove away.

Tony Meade walked quickly out into the pasture about three in the afternoon, and Roy was already twenty more posts along the fence line. Roy had barely put the maul down when Tony started talking.

"Langs'll kill us," Tony said, the sentence high-pitched at the end. Roy shrugged. "If they din't think you burnt out Mercy at first, they sure think so now. You gotta stop."

Roy looked at him, holding the handle of the maul loosely. He smiled.

"Langs don't live here no more. Don't have any-place *to* live."

"Come on," Tony said, exasperated. "They've got the truck. They've been up and down the road all day, real slow and lookin'. You gotta stop. If ya don't, I'll call the cops on ya myself."

The last words hung in the air, as if they were their own punctuation.

Then, eventually, "You won't be going to no cops," Roy said thinly. "You watched Foley's fer me. You won't be doin' nothin a'tall, less I tell ya."

Far up the river valley, a bird was kiting high on the thermals rising towards the barrens. Too far away to make out what kind of bird it actually was, just that it was alone and alert, hardly more than a speck tilting up and down in the air.

"I've got the shotgun, you know," Tony said, looking at the ground.

Roy looked at him steadily then, his hooded eyes not blinking, his face impassive. His mouth moved slightly as he chewed on a sliver of wood. A long, measuring look.

"Yeah, well." He shrugged, took out a cigarette, lit it carefully with his lighter, the flame flaring high in front of his face for a moment. "It's a long summer. You gotta sleep."

Then he lifted his chainsaw from the ground and turned it so that the chainsaw blade lay flat across his shoulder. He turned away and walked down the road next to the river towards the truck, his feet raising small dusty clouds, the maul hanging from his hand by its long handle as if it weighed nothing at all.

The juncos, small grey birds with white bibs, flew away in short, alarmed arcs out in front of him, and a dragonfly hung, almost motionless, watching. In a nearby spruce, there was the liquid burble of a robin singing. Grass met sky in an even line high above the fenceposts, and the smell of summer was full in the air. Far away, someone hammered, metal on metal, and gently, like breathing, came the roll of the swells in on the rocky beach.

Tony watched his brother start the truck and pull off down the road. And with a sudden exhaling breath sweeping up from the sea, the air abruptly felt as cold as if fall had already come.

In Between

"SHE'S BEEN IN MY HOUSE. I'LL BURN THE bitch, Charley," Brendan Connor said. Now, there's something to be frightened about, fires and rowhouses. I'd be lying if I said that most people downtown didn't think about fires at least once a week. You can't always get insurance in downtown St. John's, companies don't want to take the risk, and when there are fires, they often take houses two and three at a time. Shared walls and shared roofs, old, dry wood and no firebreaks between the floors. Like rows of flammable dominoes, windows instead of dots, just waiting to fall.

And it wasn't just Brendan who knew Mrs. Murphy.

"She's blind in one eye," the woman who sold me the house said, laughing, when I had asked about noise. "Blind in one eye and quiet as a mouse."

That, when I was trying to figure out if I really wanted to buy a house in a long row of shared walls and narrow back yards, when I was asking who the neighbours were, and whether it looked like I'd have any trouble.

It was a narrow house, one in a line of narrow rowhouses. Red. Ochre red, really — red but in that flat-toned, matte-flat old paint that so dignifies clapboard. Long, uneven ranges of clapboard along the front, and rectangular, blind windows, heavily shaded so that you can only imagine the rooms inside, rooms dark enough to hide the dust on the lampshades and what you would imagine might be fussy end-tables. Except for the fact that I have no real furniture, only an office chair and a small table, a bed and book-shelves.

Blind in one eye she was, and eye-patched, too, with a black fabric triangle like something out of a pirate movie. I wouldn't know that until several weeks after I moved in, although I would occasionally hear her on the other side of the wall, shuffling like a small mouse caught there in the air pocket behind the plaster and lathe.

Worse, still, in the bathtub. Yes, the bathtub, that porcelain parabolic ear — I'd lie there, once the water was turned off and the ripples were lapping my belly, when the house was quiet and empty, and I'd hear disconnected, scattered words, as if fistfuls of letters were making their way through the pipe chases.

"If I ... Don't."

"Telling you that it isn't..."

"Not right, not at all …"

It was never a complete sentence, rarely in fact a complete clause. But I'd hear it nonetheless and strain to make out just a few words more. It was as if she was talking intensely to someone who wasn't there. Only one voice, clearly a woman, but soft, a muttering, really, with rounded consonants so it had an eerie sibilance. Perhaps it was the walls themselves, or more precisely, the travel through the walls, that rounded the words. I don't know.

I found out her name from a bill that had been put into my mailbox accidentally: Anne Meadus Murphy. A Mrs., but with no sign of the Mr.

And then I caught her one day, watching. I was out behind the house, wandering through that most dislocating of worlds, someone else's garden left behind – peonies, big and hanging low by then, rows and rows of stubborn, unweeded perennials, tumbledown, fragrant shrub roses scattering white petals like fat confetti – watching me from what would have been the kitchen, if the geography of her house was the same as mine. Her small face in the window, the kind of face that suggests suspicion just in its construction. She had a short, sharp nose, thin mouth with lips pressed tight and pulled down in the corners, all of her features set into a face as round as a bowl. Pick one word out of the air for her, and it would be *disapproving*. I waved, and she pulled back out of sight quickly. If you hadn't seen it happen, you might imagine it was an illusion. The glass so clear and empty, flat enough to walk mere inches this side of a mirror.

I knew about Brendan Connor, the man on the other side, already – who didn't, given everything that had been said about him in the news? His house had been empty, at least until some relative could be identified to come in and strip it out, to clean it up enough that it could be put on the market. Social Services had seen to that. It looked like a smart buy, in that mercenary way, the way the '80s real estate speculators used to talk about it: you know, buy a distressed property or one on a rundown street, then move on when the neighbourhood gets fancied up.

He was, the stories said, unfit to care for himself, surrounded by rubbish and old newspapers. They took him away when they found he hadn't washed in weeks. Turner, one of the reporters from the newspaper where I worked, said there was a circle of fine dirt around every pore on his hands, so that the backs of his hands looked patterned, almost camouflaged. That his hands looked speckled, like fish skins. Connor didn't agree, and it was news for a while – that the authorities would come in and take a seventy-year-old man from his home. But when you found out more about how he was living – when Turner talked about the scores of cats and the piled, filthy dishes and the garbage simply thrown out the back into the yard, you were less sympathetic. When the neighbours talked about rats strolling the tops of their fences like tightrope walkers, well, some of the magic of renegade individualism faded.

But then, for no reason, they let Brendan come back. They let him come back, or they ran out of reasons to hold him. Or else he simply left and they didn't come looking. It's hard to know — sometimes people just manage to walk away, and it's more than the system can do to find them again. Too much paper passed through too many hands, no one directly responsible for anything, too many people with full caseloads and more important problems to solve.

I saw him at the front door with a great big handful of keys, muttering and looking for the right one. Right after I moved in, while the books were all still in boxes. And by then, Turner had told me even more about what the house was like: half-empty cans of ravioli perched on chairs, on the stairs, pretty much anywhere he had left them when he'd stopped eating and set them down. That he had piles of newspaper three and four feet high, scattered through the house, years of newsprint, yellowing and crumbling wherever it lay. An upstairs room filled with coils of green garden hose and milk crates of either rusty or greasy bicycle parts. And, by the end of the last spring, no electricity, maybe because he didn't want to pay the bills, maybe because the envelopes were just never opened. Crusted pots and pans all around a white-gas camp stove on the kitchen table.

Turner said he made his way around at night with candles, except in the summer, when he mostly slept with the dark and got up as soon as it was light, four o'clock or earlier.

When I met him, shuffling around his yard in stained, dark-grey suit pants and suspenders, his fly half-down, he called me "Charley," for no reason I could understand. My name is Stephen.

Sorry – that's right – I should have told you. My name is Stephen, Stephen Morris, and I sell classified ads for a newspaper. Pretty much all day on the telephone or at the front counter, and then home. You can't really put much romance into it, except if you tell someone in a bar that you're a newspaperman. It's a lie, sure, but a harmless one. I'm forty and single, now, and I'll try and avoid the shorthand that this would all be if I were writing my own "personals" ad in the paper. You know the kind, "swm, tidy, quiet, seeks… etc." I'm more "articles for sale" material: "For sale – dryer in working condition, two sets wooden shelves, bicycle, wedding dress size ten, never worn."

I'm old enough to have hair sprouting out of the backs of my upper arms, old enough to feel truly second-hand already – and old enough to know that the word "catch" won't ever apply to me.

I'm the kind of flotsam that's statistically supposed to exist everywhere; you know, the "two out of every three marriages" kind, the starting again, picking up the pieces kind. The kind of guy who's lugging around more baggage than he has hands to carry it with. The kind who provokes tight-lipped head shaking at parties he's not even invited to any more.

So, to put life into the same sort of shorthand: new phone number, new address, new house – smaller than the one I left, a new universe with quiet, empty, hardwood-floored rooms. But at the same time, rooms where I was comfortably alone – in every single one.

One Sunday afternoon in July, about two weeks after I moved in, I found Mrs. Murphy in my basement, standing in front of my washer. The washer lid was open, and she was staring in at the wet clothes.

"Nice day," I said.

"Is it?" she answered, staring back hard.

She's a small woman, thin, somewhere in her sixties, only five feet tall or so, but she stands like a taut wire, leaning towards you on the balls of her feet, poised. Then, that incongruous pudding-bowl face, a face that looked as if it was meant to be suited to warmth and caring and a plate of fresh muffins, but instead came across as strict and almost bulldog-tough. Pugnacious. We stood like that for a minute or two, and then she went out the back door into the yard, a door I have never unlocked, have never opened, a door I'm pretty sure I don't even have a key to. There were keys for the Yale lock and the deadbolt for the front door on the keychain the lawyer handed me after the sale closed, and another gold-coloured key that opened the back door onto the deck. Three keys and a worn leather tab, worn so smooth that you could see there used to be words pressed into the leather, now little more than shallow ridges.

And once she'd closed the door, not slamming it but pulling it closed behind her with a sudden huff of wind, it was almost as if there were no door, as if its simple white rectangle sealed tight into the white-painted back wall of the basement – and as if she had never been there at all. The kind of thing that makes you shake your head sharply, trying to clear your mind of the cobwebs of imagination.

It was not, in the end, the magic it seemed: Mrs. Murphy had lived in the neighbourhood for as long as anyone, and she had a history of feeding the cats of vacationing neighbours, bringing in the mail – and collecting door keys – but that was something I wouldn't find out from a chatty mailman until almost a year had passed.

I put the wash into the dryer, thinking about Mrs. Murphy springing over the fence between our yards like a misshapen little angry sparrow. And I decided to buy a new lock for the basement door.

Brendan was digging in his yard then, a long, narrow trench from the back right corner of his foundation. There was lumber piled next to the hole, two-by-fours and flat boards, like you'd use for concrete framing. I didn't want to ask what he was doing. He was working with a pick and shovel, wiping sweat from his forehead with an astonishingly dirty handkerchief and leaving brown streaks behind. With a morning's digging, the trench was already ten feet long, and close to three feet deep.

"You should stay off another person's ground, Charley," he said, breathing hard. "Stay off their ground, 'nless you ask 'em. That's politeness."

The soil is hard clay pan back there, full of rocks, mostly dark grey shales that threw sparks from the tip of the pick. I was leaning on the fence, looking into the thicket of timothy grass, goatweed and thistles that sprouted up between cans and rusting chunks of metal. He had a six of India beer there, three empty, three to go, and it was hot for St. John's, with a miasma coming off him that was far more than hard work and sweat. The SPCA had taken all the cats at the same time Social Services had taken Brendan, but already there were three more, watching us from his back window. His back door was open, and the back hall looked as wrecked as if the house had been abandoned: wallpaper hanging in long, mildew-speckled strips, tangles of dirty clothes on the floor. There was no reason to believe that anyone, even Mrs. Murphy, would want to go in there. While I watched, one of the cats came out into the hallway, tail flicking, and pounced on something out of sight from where I was standing.

"Watch out for her," Brendan said, sweaty circles blossoming on his collared shirt, in under his arms and in the middle of his back. "She's bad trouble." He was wearing dirty sneakers with the laces pulled loose, the tongues reaching up in the air as if his feet were too swollen to be packed into the sneaker tops. He swung the pick as if he were accustomed to it, hands sliding just far enough along the handle as the pick swept through its descending arc. Then he'd raise it again, loose-elbowed, relaxed, an ease of motion in his movements. Enough to see that it was a motion he was more than familiar with.

"Strange 'uns around here," he grunted. "You should be careful. Old woman over there" – he waved one hand loosely toward a green house with yellow trim, then grabbed the pick handle again – "she just screams all the time. No reason fer it a'tall."

I wanted to ask what he was doing with the wood, with the trench, but it just didn't seem polite. Then, the next morning, around four a.m., the hammering started, and one by one the other neighbours started to wake up and realize that Brendan was home.

I WOKE UP THE NEXT NIGHT, convinced that serious, small, half-blind Mrs. Murphy was standing at the foot of the bed, her mouth a thin line, but by the time I could find the light switch and turn the light on, the room was empty. There wasn't a single sound of her in the house, not a footstep or the distinctive whisper of fabric, only the occasional creak of the house cooling, the flat-top black roof surrendering the day's heat back to the chill of the night.

By then, I was starting to be at home in the house the way you become, able to trace my way around the rooms without turning on any lights at night, knowing where everything was, about how many footsteps it was from doorway to doorway, and there was a familiar feel to the place. The shape of the empty living room with its three bow windows – the room behind that, with the addition of a table and chairs, might become a dining room. The sound the refrigerator made, coming on. I couldn't tell you how many steps there were in the single long flight of hardwood stairs, but my legs suddenly knew when I was at the top or the bottom even if my head didn't, knew when to take that first flat step.

And Brendan got to the end of one long trench, and turned at right angles, and started digging again.

Every day, six more brown bottles of India would empty, after Brendan picked them up down at the store with his thin roll of real old bills from somewhere inside his clothes, and each day, the trench got longer. Brendan turned again, puffing, sweating, starting back towards the other corner of the foundation. You could tell it was old grass, well-rooted, that the sods only gave up to the shovel after plenty of effort. The roots of the goatweed ran everywhere, naked and white when they were turned up in the sun, tangling and twisting, strangling the other plants from beneath.

"New back porch. Gonna be like Fort Knox," Brendan said. "See if she can get in now, evil old cow. More locks on it than even the Devil can make keys for."

Once the forms were built, he started making concrete in a wheelbarrow. Using the hose from the side of my house for water. I met him once coming down the street with a 50-pound bag of cement across his shoulders like he'd trapped some strange, heavy and legless prey, and was bringing it home for dinner. He was miles – easily miles – from anywhere you could buy cement.

He mixed and dumped, mixed and dumped, drank India and sweated.

"Got a permit?" I asked, worried about what the city would make of this strange, piecemeal construction of a foundation, not even deep enough to reach beneath the frost line.

"Shhh. Don't let her hear that, Charley," Brendan said, looking over towards Mrs. Murphy's yard. You could see her there, flitting, trimming, scissors in her grip, gardening gloves on her too-small hands. "Turned me in to Social Services, she did. Told 'em I was a danger to th' neighbours. Not enough to be fishing around in my stuff, she wanted it all to herself."

What a wild kaleidoscope of a thought that was — that anyone would want anything from that house. Even on a still day, you could smell the mildew from the back.

People deal with separation differently, I know. Some blow up, turning it all into a jumbo, two-way war. Others shrivel, aging and wrinkling right there in front of you as if they were holding psychic radium in their bare hands, caving in like someone's cheeks when their false teeth have been taken out. Me? I could lie on my bed and stare at the ceiling for hours, absolutely no fight left in me, as empty as if someone had opened a vein and drained out every drop of will. Watching the shadows of the leaves against the walls and ceiling, amazed sometimes about things as simple as the telephone on the floor near the bed — amazed that it seemed I had never, ever heard it ring.

I heard the faucets in my kitchen. Brendan had his shirt off, and he was noisily washing his face and hands in the stainless steel sink. Splashing water around all over, like a defiant little bird in a birdbath. Later, I'd find a small delta of silt and sand near the open circle of the drain. "You're a nice fella, Charley," Brendan said, his voice muffled in my dishcloth. "Fella who can be trusted. Not like some."

Trusted: right. And, sure, the wheels fell off then, but they're bound to fall off eventually.

When the dreams start, when you start questioning everything about how a marriage breaks down. The dreams where everything was all right, and the dreams where everything goes wrong. I dreamt she cut her hair short, right to the scalp, and I had small, tufts of that cut hair in my hands, feeling it soft between my fingertips, until she ordered me to turn around. "You're not allowed to look at me," she said. The dreams where I am making love to her, until suddenly, there are teeth involved, and I find all at once that my hands are strangely gone, replaced by waxy stumps. Sometimes, I wake up and realize I've really lost something. You don't remember the way things hurt, so the heat of anger eventually fades to the slow simmer of regret.

And, oh, when the wheels fall off, it's far from pretty.

I know there's a place in downtown St. John's where the top of the bar is a sheet of flat copper, and I know that when you're drunk enough, it feels cool and wonderfully welcoming against the side of your face. That you can only do that when no one's looking, when no one's paying attention, or they'll give you your walking papers right there and then. So you look both ways – "Look, look mom, I'm crossing the street safe!" – and if nothing's coming, you put your face down. And you can smell that rich, sharp, green copper smell, the same way your hands smell after you've been handling copper pipe. My own little voodoo supplication, like the copper bracelets some people wear to cure arthritis. But you only get a moment — it's best to make it look like you've dropped something on the floor, something you can't quite reach with the tips of your fingers.

And those nights lead to hard mornings. In an empty house, there's little to trip over on your way to the bathroom, few things you can smack into and start to bleed. The faucets, maybe, when you try to splash cold water on your face, and cruelly misjudge the distance between your head and the chrome. The doorframe, when you bang straight into it, starting to walk without properly opening your eyes — but there's no shame in that. Any more than there's someone to be embarrassed for you — or ashamed of you — when it takes nine or ten times to get your keys into the front door lock. Or when you drop the keys. Drop the keys, and just can't seem to pick them up.

And sometimes I'd be standing there with the keys finally back in my hand, head in sparkles with the sudden movement of standing upright again, and I'd have that crawling feeling between my shoulder blades, that feeling that someone was looking at me.

Leaning on the fence on another weekend day, watching Brendan finish another beer and drop the empty brown bottle back into the box. Watching Mrs. Murphy, shuttling like a beetle, down to the bottom of her yard and back, watching her hang laundry on the line, staring across hard at us, challengingly, before she began to hang up the underwear and socks.

"So what happened?" I asked.

"Husband broke her eyesocket wit' his fist. She lost the eye." There was something about his voice, then. The only time I had heard Brendan even remotely sympathetic for Mrs. Murphy, but only for the briefest moment.

"Mean drunk he was. Livin' with her, you might unnerstand it."

The way Brendan told the story, Mrs. Murphy's husband had worked at the dockyard, painting and sandblasting the big factory-freezer trawlers, until collapsing scaffolding had brought him suddenly and dramatically to earth. She'd nursed him for the months that he'd been left in bed, and then tolerated him for the months after, when he had started investing his disability checks in rye. Tiny though she was, Brendan said she could lug her husband up the stairs from the front door – at least until he woke up one night while she was taking off his socks, swung his fist once, and promptly passed out again while she lay bleeding on the floor.

And that was when I realized, or at least I decided, that there wasn't one single person left on the planet who actually cared what happened to me. Sure, I have brothers who moved to the mainland for work, and parents – old now – who live in Seattle and concentrate on their garden – but I can't imagine a thing I could say to any of them that would get them angry enough to even think of hitting me. That's a strange way to think of it, sure – but there it is. Nothing you do matters, because it doesn't end up affecting anyone.

That's the centre of it, you know; you can watch other people spiral down, watch them on their flaming, smoking spins, their hard, definite intersection with solid ground, and ask yourself why they don't do anything to save themselves. Why they don't lift a finger. Why they refuse to swim, and seem to consciously decide to sink. And outside of it, you can shake your head and say that it's sad, that they're just self-destructing for meaningless reasons, just letting themselves go.

Inside, it's more complicated. I know I have the feeling that, away from the easy, slick surfaces of casual conversation, I'm of no more importance than a laboratory experiment, the equivalent of watching to see how fast bread molds. "Look, look, now he's forgotten to shave. Better write that down." Work skids, and in the lunch room, they're taking odds on how many weeks I've got left before someone pulls the plug.

Sitting in the yard, drinking beer with Brendan. I figured I'll have hit bottom when we're actually sharing a bottle. Maybe by then, I wouldn't have to worry about work.

"So what's next?" I asked. I must have said it out loud: Brendan must have misunderstood.

"After this? Terraces," Brendan said. "Gonna build terraces. Wit' annuals. For when she's prowlin' around in my yard. Mebbe in the dark, she'll fall off and break her freakin' neck."

It was later in the summer then, and the fireweed that had sprung up all around the bottom of Brendan's yard had gone to seed, long, filmy ribbons hanging from the pods, waiting for the first breath of wind to draw them away to find some other open ground. The stringers were all up for the new porch with wood he'd salvaged. Some pieces new, others left over and torn down from someone else's reconstruction project, still studded with plaster nails and the occasional torn corner of gyprock wallboard. He'd been scrounging plywood for the walls, and it was stacked against the side of the house, some of it laced with staples from where it had been the backdrop for bar posters.

I admit things were falling apart by then. That Brendan didn't even smell so bad any more, that maybe, objectively, I smelled just as bad, that we could spend much of the day half in the bag, digging into whatever plan he had that day. Pounding nails and pounding fingers, swearing and dropping things, following through on things that didn't really lead anywhere. Using up all my sick days at work, because I couldn't be bothered to go in. Unplugging the phone, when the office became my first and only regular home telephone caller.

Then one more night, one more copper-faced, slab-sided night, I was coming back up the street from downtown and I stopped by Brendan's, where a feeble light shone in one downstairs window.

I'd already had my usual night of blind hope and pragmatic despair. The bar is noisy on Fridays, much of the light from tangled ropes of small Christmas lights that stay up along the ceiling all year round like multi-coloured constellations. There are two regular bartenders, one blonde, one brunette, and they wear tight tops that bare perfectly soft and smooth stomachs.

They are like small, jewelled, uncatchable tropical birds, thin-waisted and devastatingly pretty, and they flit back and forth, serving customers along the whole length of the metal bar. Every single night, I imagine holding one or the other of them in my arms, but they smile and speak to me only when it's obviously time for a refill.

"How are you doing?" the blonde one says brightly, and a long explanation springs into my head that I can't begin to say, and that, in truth, she has no interest in listening to.

When she turns her back to me, I stare unabashedly at her and imagine dancing with her.

But they'd no more consider dancing with me than they would dance with bedraggled Brendan, stinking of must and with his shirt-tails tufting out through the front of his trousers.

So every night, just like this one, I dream hopelessly before staggering out to reality.

Walking home, I remember thinking that the rooflines of the rowhouses looked like their shoulders were slumping – the eyes of their windows still wide, but also resigned.

Bleary-eyed, looking in through Brendan's ragged curtains, the only thing I could see at first was his candle, guttering on a table next to a pile of newspapers. And I could understand the neighbours' fears, why they thought Brendan might well burn down the whole block any day now. Then I could make out the shape of his sleeping body, stretched across a bursting, tufted sofa, his feet still packed into his sneakers, one foot up on the table, nudged up against the lit candle. And I could see the beer bottles, six or eight, strewn sideways on the floor, all near his hand, trailing on the carpet. Then I saw someone else in the room – Anne Murphy, with something in her hands.

I got one more wink, just one short glimpse before the candle was blown out. One short, incredible image flashed against my retinas so it stayed there like a ridiculous and unbelieveable afterimage. Anne Meadus Murphy from next door, spreading a blanket over Brendan's soundly-sleeping body. Tucking him in, though he gave no sign of knowing she was even there.

It took me ages to get into the house that night. I couldn't get the keys to work, so I sat on the front steps, eventually lying back for a while to look at the stars. There aren't as many stars in the city as there were where I used to live, I remember thinking that. The orange of the streetlights rubs away the weaker ones like an eraser on paper; at my old house, you could look up and see the delicate sweep of the whole Milky Way, watch the fall of the Perseid and the Leonid meteors, lie under a million stars burning like bright diamonds in the black. At my new house, head out of the clouds, I could watch one of Brendan's cats, stalking the night-wandering, sky-stumbling moths – and then eating them.

I got into the house eventually. If you hold your breath and concentrate, sometimes that gives you enough control to make the tip of the key stop shaking. I dropped my jacket at the foot of the stairs and stuffed my keys back into my left pocket – there are some things that stay in order, like where you put your toothbrush, and which cupboards hold the glasses, and which ones the plates.

Then, somewhere halfway up, my feet forgot just how many stairs there really were.

She must have heard me fall from the other side of the wall, must have heard me hit the bare hardwood at the foot of the stairs. Because when I opened my eyes, the side of my face already swelling from where I had hit the floor, Mrs. Murphy was kneeling right in front of me, holding a mug. And I still have no idea how she kept getting into my house.

"Tea," she said quietly, smiling. "Just tea." She had more concern in one eye than most people have in both for me lately.

I'd like to say that I threw open the curtains the next day and shouted out that it was a new world, a new and wonderful world. But I don't have any curtains upstairs yet, so I celebrated morning by squinting my eyes shut against the latest hangover, rolling over and burying my face in the pillow until after noon. And, over and over again, feeling the throb of my badly-bruised face like a taut little drum, hit hard with every heartbeat.

When I did get up, it was hot outside, the sun blazing the way it does for far too few St. John's summer days.

Hot Tub

AT THREE IN THE AFTERNOON, THE SUN blazing, John climbed into the hot tub and felt the gentle fizz of the bubbles catching on the dark hairs of his legs and arms and on the fine, almost-invisible hairs on his back. He felt the heat of the water move in toward his bones; it almost seemed to bounce back out again through the tissue, warming as much coming out as it had moving in.

There were kids in the nearby pool, three dark-haired kids from Quebec — he had heard them talking in French to their mother, who lay on a beach chair under the sun, diligently working sunscreen into her long, slender arms. Three dark-haired kids like cut-out versions of the same person at different ages, looping through the water like otters, going over and under the line of blue and white floats that separated the deep end from shallower water. Watching over the edge of the hot tub, he could see the woman had long fingers, too, watched as the fingers followed the contours of her arms and shoulders.

John's kids were over at the rented cabin, fighting and watching television, too big now really for cabin vacations, big enough to be surly and to roll their eyes, big enough to be on the edge of being actively-disagreeable adults.

He had discussed this with Heather before they left. He was excited enough about the idea of recapturing the fun of old vacations that he had carried on about it for more than a week, his words fast and almost without punctuation, excited enough that he hadn't realized that he was the only one paying attention. Heather had thought the trip a bad idea, saying he was trying to make up for time hopelessly lost, trying to recreate time he had wasted through inattention, and that the children, one now a teenager and the other twelve, would not be the laughing, beach-loving kids he seemed to be expecting. But, uncharacteristically, he had forced the issue, made the plans and booked the cabin, talked excitedly about how much fun it would be, even while the other three had taken turns telling him he was wrong, that it was a bad idea, that, like so many of his ideas, it was destined to fail.

And now it seemed like they were right, because it had unravelled quickly into fighting in the too-small cabin, bickering first over who would get which bed, and tumbling downhill from there to the easy, sibling back-and-forth that is both effortless to take part in and exhausting to listen to.

Four o'clock, and he watched Heather walk evenly across the grass towards the enclosure where the outdoor swimming pool and hot tub were, the hot tub up high enough so that he could easily see over the fence. He could tell his wife was angry by the way she pointed her toes inwards with every step, purposefully putting each foot down in line, like a cat's tracks in shallow snow. She was looking at the ground, walking the anger tightrope, wound up tight as a drum. And he knew why, this time, knew she was frustrated that he was in the hot tub while she was at the cabin, and he could imagine the kids fighting offhandedly, her irritation growing as sharp as the sound of a knife drawn hard against a plate. He watched her come in through the gate, carefully latch it, and walk to the edge of the hot tub without even putting a step out of line. It was, he thought, beautiful, but in a dangerous way, like plum-coloured flames skipping toward you across spilled gasoline.

"Come back over to the barbecue," she said quietly, smiling. "Come back over to the barbecue and I'll get you a beer from the fridge." But he didn't answer, looking at the ruler-straight line of green that was the front edge of a farmer's field across from the cabins. Wheat, he thought, or maybe oats. Maybe oats; he didn't know. Forty-one years old, he thought, and I don't know wheat from damned oats.

Heather leaned in close to him.

"Get out of the fucking hot tub," she whispered quickly and angrily, her face turned away from the swimming pool so the kids from Quebec couldn't hear her. "Get out of the fucking hot tub and get back to the cabin, and we'll talk about it there." John wondered about her face then, wondered if the skin under her eyes always got darker when she was really angry. He was studying her like she was a science experiment, not like her face belonged to someone he knew, and he realized it was only the three otters in the pool that were keeping her from exploding.

When she walked away, he could tell by each line of her body, by the precise straight swing of her arms, by the way she was holding her shoulders, that she was beyond furious. That she was so angry that she was depending on the rigidity of her body to maintain control over her temper. He could almost hear the words zinging around her head, "So stay there. You can drown for all I care."

By six, still floating, he had figured out that it must be a hawk that was hanging in the sky over the field, hanging up there with its wings peaked like surprised eyebrows, swaying slowly back and forth on the shifting thermal updrafts. John wondered what it was the hawk was seeing, whether the bird was focusing on one small patch in the field, or whether it was looking across the whole panorama beneath it, seeing as part of the view a pale man banked against the light blue side of the hot tub, seeing the three children as they left the pool with their mother, closing the gate behind them. She had come over to the hot tub before that, surprising John, asking him how hot the water was, trailing her fingertips in the bubbles for a moment. She called out goodbye when the gate was closing. Someone was mowing grass – he could hear the distant, regular purr of the mower, although he couldn't see it, and occasional breaths of wind brought the clear, sweet smell of the cut grass. It was the time in summer when seconds drag and minutes trail, when the day limps weakly towards evening under the weight of the summer heat.

It was even hotter in the tub: John could feel the fat beads of sweat rolling out of his hairline, rolling down his cheeks and narrowly missing the corners of his eyes. Now and then, he'd lay his arms on the deck, and once, he stood up to pull a towel over towards him. The sudden movement made him dizzy for a moment, stars and snow jumping in front of his eyes – he twisted the plastic cap from the big bottle of water, and drank deeply.

Two families came out to play a game of catch in the grassy open field directly beside the pool fence, kids and parents and a ball and bat, and even with his eyes closed John could picture the loosely-played game, could hear the hard wooden thwack of the bat and the rush of feet, the crowded, eager yells of children scrambling for the ball.

The robins started their late, liquid songs, and the ball players left, and still Heather didn't come back. He had heard her call his name once or twice, short, sharp yells, cut off abruptly like someone calling a disobedient pet. John. John. Then a door slamming, hard.

By nine, the sun was tilting down. Sky orange along the horizon, the upwards-reaching arms of the trees suddenly and sharply jet black, branches set so sharply against the sky that they were matte and completely without depth, just simple cut-outs pasted up against the whorled depth of the sky. The pool was lit up blue in the fading evening, the white underwater lights playing off the blue-painted bottom, the brightness of the water sharpening with each subtle darkening of the sky, until the lights made it glow electric and unnatural. Strings of coloured patio lights wobbled along the fence top, teetering in the slightest breeze. To John, the water surrounding him no longer felt hot, hardly even warm, and not because it was cooling. By then, the skin on his hands and feet felt waterlogged, and he could imagine his feet, naked and stark-white and horrendously wrinkled, soft as sponges and never again needed for walking.

I am, he thought, acclimatizing, learning to live in the heat like the peculiar sea-bottom bacteria that thrive around volcanic fumeroles.

Fumeroles, he thought. What a strange word, what an awkward word, to have stuck in memory, to be remembered instead of discarded like so many others. He could picture a fumerole from some once-watched nature special, videotape shot through the thick glass eyepiece of a deep-diving submersible, the hot water and silt boiling up like smoke. He let his back slide down until his chin reached the water, then pulled his whole body under. I am a submarine, he thought, diving to the fumeroles. But at the last moment he decided not to open his eyes, and came back up to the surface gasping when his breath ran out. The water that ran into his eyes stung like fire.

At eleven, they turned off the lights between the cabins, and the stars suddenly sprang out in the sky. He could hear the fizz of the water, and smell the alkali-chlorine hot-springs breath of it. Heather had given up calling by then. She clearly planned to wait him out instead, and the echoes of other daytime voices had long since stopped ringing off the sides of the cabins.

Fire pits were lit in front of some of the cabins now, burning sappy wood that snapped and cracked and filled the air with a thin grey smoke that smelled strongly of pine. Slab wood, the bark-covered, outside-edge leftovers from sawmill lumber, rough-cut and splintery and dry as dust, and, from around the fires, John could hear low voices, fragments of conspiratorial sentences, tossed out haphazardly from the chairs grouped around the small pools of firelight.

"Right over the green, and he said..."

"I couldn't believe..."

"Just one more time and I would have said 'No way, you're gone,' but..."

They were soft words, almost murmurs, escaping only occasionally from the fire's edge as if each individual syllable had tunneled its way out under the blanket of darkness.

His attention was wandering – his body strangely heavy and his face felt flushed with sunburn. The water bottle was more than half empty. He hung his arms out over the edge of the hot tub, watched them loll, over-fat, fleshy and almost beyond his control. He imagined himself as a drowned man, caught in the ebb and flow of the tide, seaweed and sea-wrack all around him. He could imagine lying limp in the Irish moss washed up at the edge of the ocean, the delicate, rolled edges of the pink seaweed curled around him, the iodine smell thick in the air, face up to the sun and the blue sky. He could feel how the shallow, lapping waves would lift his ankles, then the rest of his body, could hear their light, open-handed slap against the shore.

Perhaps two early beach-walkers, wearing serious walking shoes and multi-pocketed khaki shorts, would be the first to find him. Big, safe, sun-shielding, sensible hats, sunglasses dangling on strings, they would be faced by the wreckage left behind after the shrimp and the seagulls and the crab and lobster had all taken their turn at his exposed flesh. He could imagine their shock and horror, how they would step back and hunt in their pockets for the handy efficiency of a cellphone. In his imagination, John drew limply-flapping yellow police tape around himself on the beach, sand grains thick in his hair and in the corners of whatever might be left of his eyes.

And then a different thought: he imagined Heather and the kids walking along the beach, walking above the tide line on the ruled-flat, fine sand, their footprints webbed out behind them, their eyes downcast, faces serious, as if they expected to find something important in all that sand. He imagined them walking and walking, their steps stretching out behind them in ever-longer sentences of explanation and regret, rambling words unspoken, unheard, unread.

As the lights inside the cabins were winking out, he began to smile – a thin, hard smile that made his mouth seem all wrong inside the round softness of his face.

By two in the morning, lit only by the single streetlight near the outdoor phone, he was asleep, lulled by the gentle whirr of the pump, bubbles coming up in waves under his armpits, lingering across his chest. Almost floating, he dreamt about rain, about the ditches filling quickly with fast brown water, about the brush on both sides of the road heavy with rain, branches trailing down to the ground. The ditch water overflowing, forcing itself into culverts. Branches and small uprooted trees rushed by in the flowing water and, in his dream, he could hear the sibilant speech of the gravel wicking over the ridges in the metal culverts. The water was undercutting the edge of the road's shoulder, then sweeping away falls of gravel that toppled into the water. Small rocks hissed and sang, and the water pulling down into the culverts built brown sucking whirlpools capped with dirty round hats of brown-flecked foam. And in the dream, he swept through the culverts and rushed towards the sea himself, bouncing over the short falls in the ditches and fleeing into the stream that ran deep and silt-dirty under the road to the river, going exactly where he was sent by the rushing waters, arms and legs limp and dancing in the ridges and valleys of the waves. There was no point grabbing at the trees along the sides of the water; he knew that they would either give way or his hands would fail to get a proper grip, that the effort of getting out of the water would be profoundly exhausting.

While he slept, a late-night thunder storm grumbled off to the west of the cabins, big clouds piled high and grey against the night, backlit by the occasional flash and wink of lightning, the kind of storm whose laconic travel along the horizon ticks like nature's clock, measuring with soft and imprecise strokes.

And he dreamt about the woman from Quebec, dreamt that he knew her, that he should know her name, that it should come to him unbidden at the simple memory of the brush strokes that shaped her face. But her name stayed disturbingly out of reach, a feathery thought that would not allow itself to be grasped.

He dreamt that she came to the pool, alone, stepping with long, incautious steps, and walked to where he lay, his head canted back against the side of the hot tub. That she reached out and ran a long, cool fingertip across the curve of his upper lip, over that shallow valley directly beneath his nostrils; all the time without speaking, just smiling gently. And he smelled a fragrance he had not smelled since high school, a perfume that he could always place and never remember having smelled again, the perfume the wife of his grade 12 English teacher used to wear. Tall and willowy, she had always seemed to move without walking, had seemed to float past the enraptured high school boys before they were even in a position to recognize the magic of her motion.

But when he opened his eyes, there was only the black, cool night and the gentle fizz of the sounds in his ears. This time, he knew he was smiling. And this time, he knew why.

Dawn often starts as a grey line on the morning after a sunny day, a grey starting that widens like an eye opening slowly from sleep in a familiar room. Then the arc of the sky blues, ever so slightly, and the periphery of stars begins to fade, leaving only the most energetic behind. The first birds start to sing awkwardly, throwing out fragments of their songs, as if every morning they have to learn the full melody all over again. The streetlights turn off, one by one, their sensors snapping away their pools of orange light, and the sky fills with light like singers singing. The gradient lightens from the bottom up, and the blues of the sky develop as if they were photographs gently rocking in a tray of darkroom developing fluid.

By the time John woke up, the sky had rinsed itself to blue. When he opened his eyes, the caretaker, an odd-looking thin man with a small head and arms too long for his body, was skimming leaves from the surface of the pool with a long-handled white net.

John saw that the caretaker was staring at him, and lifted one wet, puffy hand in an awkward wave. And the caretaker took one hand from the net and waved back, and then quickly looked away, scooping up the leaves and the struggling insects that had been lured into the pool by the rippling nighttime lights.

Looking towards the cabins, he could see the woman from Quebec hanging beach towels over the railings on the deck behind her cabin. The quadrangle of grass was empty, except for a small flock of starlings hopping along, bending their heads and pecking fitfully at the ground. She turned towards him, and smiled a knowing smile, the kind of smile that is more a shared answer than a question. With one long finger, she touched her upper lip.

And he knew then that he was rushing towards the surface, still able to feel and touch, that while his skin felt waterlogged and heavy, he hadn't really drowned. Not yet. He lifted himself out of the water, feeling the air on his skin and the ordered sense of muscles and bones moving as he stood up and climbed over the edge of the hot tub. The water streamed down his skin, staining the brown wood of the stairs. With deliberate effort, he took that strange and unfamiliar first step.

On Call

"YOU CAN'T BE TOO CAREFUL," HE SAID, AND he put the knife right in front of my face. He was right. You can't.

It's funny how my head works at times like that – I measure, examine. Useless information – a flick knife, about four inches long, blade with a channel, wooden handle held together with brass rivets. Blade long enough to permanently damage internal organs – liver, spleen, lungs, heart. Long enough to do slapdash punctures through roping yards of intestine, long enough to nick the jugular or aorta on its knifely travels, long enough to open a femoral artery, the big leg bleeder.

I'm always doing that – prepping for what comes next, trying to visualize the damage you don't have time to get tests to confirm.

I should have been thinking "walk slowly for the door, get away," but instead, I was assembling information – still diagnosing. I should have been thinking about why we didn't have panic buttons in the examining rooms, and why I was in there alone with him, anyway.

Sometimes you get an early hint. And he gave me one – I've been an emergency room doctor for enough years now, and usually the first clue is early in the workup, while the door's still open and no one has their clothes off yet.

His was right inside the door, the first few words already filled out on his chart.

"Name – Miller, Robert."

You try to jolly them along, sometimes, try to get them away from focusing on their symptoms. Especially when they've been waiting a long time, and this guy had been.

"How are you tonight, Robert?"

"Don't call me that," he said. The tone of his voice should have said it all.

"That's not your name?" I asked – I hate it when the triage nurse gets it wrong.

"That's the name *they* gave me. My real name is Elephra." He spelled it for me – it wasn't the name on his medicare card, clipped right there at the top of his chart.

Wind it all back and I should have known right there. I should have stuck my head out the door and gotten one of the big orderlies, the guys whose uniform shirts strain at the buttonholes all across their chests, the guys who like putting the wild ones into restraints. But I didn't – and that was the first mistake.

The second mistake was purely positional. Picture a hospital examining room, door in one corner, everything pretty much white, the gurney – you know, the bed you sit on – in the middle of the room, cupboards with everything from stitches to basins to bandages. The big light overhead. If I'd been thinking, you see, I'd have been on the door side of the examining table, facing him. Any doubts at all, have your back to the door – it gives you a couple of steps, anyway, a chance to get out into the hall and to start yelling at the top of your lungs.

But I'd walked to the other side, with my back to the cupboards. He was between me and the door I'd closed so he could take off his shirt and show me his back.

I'm not a big guy, maybe 5' 10" in my socks, handsome in that "he's a doctor so he makes lots of money" kind of way. When I take my face apart in the mirror, though, I always think that too many parts are just too much – nose too big, eyes too far apart, eyelashes long enough for a woman but kind of dopey-looking on me.

But that's beside the point.

I shouldn't have been so easily cornered, but I was off my game – I was tired. For that, I blame the trombone player. And the coronary from earlier that night – he hadn't made it – the two drunks who fought with beer bottles "just like in the movies" and had more open bleeders on their faces than you'd normally see in a month. The lady with the kidney stones who was screaming even though we'd laced her up on Demerol.

I was double-shifted, too, because we were short on doctors and I'd agreed to work two, back to back. That can really drain you. The right combination of nights, and you can fall asleep in the cafeteria, face-down in the scrambled eggs.

But back to Miller. I just refuse to call this guy Elephra.

He said he was a taxi driver, that his car had slid side-ways in snow down a St. John's hill, fetching up hard against a light pole. Not much of a margin in the taxi business, so there are a lot of clapped-out, repainted old cop cars with lousy tires. The kind of car where the engine warning light stays on permanently, so the driv-ers stick a piece of masking tape over it so they don't have to think about it. The drivers aren't much better.

Yeah, I hear what you're thinking. Another reason to be paying attention.

So Miller had smashed up a cab, and now his back hurt. He said it had been injured before.

I had him take off his shirt and his sweater and then he said he had to take his pants off, too, to show me where it hurt, and he spilled everything out of his pockets. Out of one front pocket, change – I remem-ber a balled-up five-dollar bill – and car keys. From the other, the knife.

One minute, things were normal – well, as normal as a hospital emergency room gets in the middle of the night, and the next I had this big knife in my face. And it wasn't completely like a threat, although it was threatening. He didn't say he was going to cut me up, just held it there as if showing me the possibilities.

Not for long. He put it down on the end of the examining table, but the blade was still open, and not far from reach.

Then he started to tell me about his daughter.

"I didn't know I had a daughter," he said, "because the doctors" – he underlined the word, I didn't – "said I couldn't have kids, but then I saw a girl on the street one day and when she looked at me, I knew I was looking at my daughter. You have kids, doc?"

Yes, I told him, not quite lying, a boy and a girl.

"And you know they're your kids the minute you look at 'em, right?"

That kind of seized me up right there. It didn't matter, though. He just kept talking.

"That's when I knew, and I tried to figure it out in reverse, you know, figure out how it was possible. I'd had the test and the doctors said I was sterile, that there was nothing there at all, so they must have been wrong again. And my girlfriend didn't tell me she was pregnant, and then I was gone to Alberta because, you know, we just started pissing each other off, and her mother, man, her mother was a piece of goods – always in my face about the smoking and the weed, so it just seemed easier to start fresh somewhere else, even if it was Calgary. But it should be against the law not to tell someone he's a father, right doc? Right?"

"Right." Sometimes, it's easier just to agree. He'd broken off talking, and he was looking at me kind of sideways, his head tilted.

"Are you a blue?" he asked suddenly.

Now, what's the safest way to answer that question? I just shrugged, hoping he'd find the answer to be obvious.

"You look like a blue to me," he said. "I can usually tell. That's good."

"That's good?"

"Yeah, good. Would have been different if you were a red. But I can see there's a lot going on with you, doc. A lot going on."

I made myself busy then, taking pages of meaningless notes, and I looked at his back, since that was what he had come in for. It seemed normal enough – tender when I prodded around, but he still had pretty good range of motion. He turned when I talked to him from behind, turned enough so that I could see that he was turning his head, not his whole upper body. Usually, the pain will stop you if anything's been torn in there.

"Spine's fused," he said.

I looked, but there weren't any signs on his back that he'd had surgery – no scars, not even a stitch here or there. Sometimes scars can fade to quite fine lines, but nobody's perfect, and you almost always see a loop or two, a place where a stitch has gone too far before being pulled tight. So, spinal fusion? Not possible.

I was beginning to think – hell, I already knew – the guy was psychotic, or at least delusional. Didn't know any more about the specifics, because it wasn't really an emergency room thing – but I thought if I could get past him, I could at least rally the troops and get him sent upstairs for a psych exam. Or at least I could get a few of the bigger guys to pin him down so they could get the knife.

"How about we get an x-ray of that back, have a look and see what's exactly going on in there?" I moved towards the door.

"I don't like x-rays," he told me, his hand reaching across the sheet. "Doctors don't know how to read them."

Then he said he had been left alone in the examining room the first time he hurt his back, with the x-rays up on the big light box in front of him.

That he had turned the light on, and had seen everything the doctor had missed.

"Inside my ribcage, you know, there's a calcified fetus," he said, his eyes wide. "Never even knew it was there, but clear as can be on the x-ray. And under my shoulder blade, there's a fishhook – just a plain fishhook, and I got no idea how it got in there."

He dug his fingers in under his armpit – "I can't even feel the bugger. But the doctors didn't see any of it. It's like they can't see what's right in front of their faces."

There was a singsong quality to his voice, a sort of hypnotic rhythm. Sometimes a person's voice gets that way when they tell a familiar story, one they've told many times before. Like the one where you drive your suv head-on into someone else's car because you're driving too fast and you're way too tired. And you're the only one in your family who even gets to walk away, and you go over it and over it with the cops and the lawyers and your parents and your wife's parents, too.

Like that.

It was really hard to pay attention to Miller. Hard to focus on what he was saying about police officers following him, about the cab company's owners wanting him to deliver liquor, about everything else. The words were just blurring.

I couldn't help it. I was tired.

Hell, I was already tired when I came on shift.

See, I live in an apartment right now and in apartments, you're always at the mercy of the neighbours. You can complain when they're noisy, of course, but that often makes things worse, and most people just can't seem to fathom what a 24-hour emergency room shift is like.

Sometimes, that kind of shift is a whole night of next to nothing – picking broken glass out of tumbledown drunks, and sprains that need nothing more than ice and pressure bandages. You get a fair amount of sleep, and only get woken up occasionally to write a prescription for strep throat or for painkillers.

Other times, it's flat out from the moment you get to the hospital, and every time you turn around, there's another car crash or a great huge knife wound where you have to spend a couple of hours just making sure you pick up all the nerve and tissue damage so some idiot doesn't turn around in three months and sue you silly. Sue you, because you patched him up after a knife fight, and now he's only got half a smile.

And the trombone player in the apartment next door to me is driving me mad. He's been there a month now, in addition to the people downstairs who work night shifts and put their laundry in at the strangest of times. I've complained to the landlord, but they can't seem to pin the guy down – it's like cops, they're never there when you need them, and this guy, he never seems to be playing when the landlord comes around.

At first, I thought he was right next door – I'd wake up and hear him as if he was in the room with me. But go out in the hall, and it's hard to find where exactly the sound is coming from. When I talk to the landlord on the phone, I can practically hear the shrug coming right back at me over the phone lines. I don't even think he believes me that the guy is there.

As for the trombone player himself, I don't know if he just doesn't realize how thin the walls are, or if he's trying to push me over the edge. Or whether he just doesn't care. He plays scales, fractured scales – one, two, three, four, five, one two, three, four, five – over and over again. Sometimes the same song – *Blue Moon* – so that, for a day or two, it peals in my head like ringing bells. You must know that old Sinatra classic – "Blue moon, you saw me standing alone ..." I'm pretty sure he's playing it with a mute – and that he knows just how loud the trombone is, and that he's making at least some effort to muffle the sound. But not enough effort, because I can be in the apartment trying to sleep and he can drive me right back into my clothes and out onto the street.

The noise is so pervasive that I've made up my own image of the guy – I assume it's a guy, although I've never seen him.

I picture him as late middle aged, paunchy and standing there playing the trombone naked, with a roaring great erection. He can play naked at home – in my imagination, that gives him some kind of charge. I don't want to think what that says about my head – I'm no expert, I only spent one rotation in psychiatry as an intern, just enough to know that it was all my mother's fault. Hey, I'm kidding, all right?

For sure, though, I'm not known for my pysch skills. They brought me the guy they call the Major once, wanted me to commit him permanently. Two police officers, and a slew of angry firemen to boot. The Major was a favourite trick they used to play on the new guys, the probationary firefighters. The fire alarm would get pulled at the Major's nursing home, always around ten at night, and the trucks would pull up and the firefighters would put the new guys in breathing gear and send them inside. They'd crawl up the stairs to the alarm station, and there'd be the Major. Uniform hat and jacket, one hand at his forehead, saluting.

He'd be staring at the spinning red lights flashing though the windows, and whacking off with his other hand.

Funny stuff, hey? At ten o'clock at night, maybe.

But not at three in the morning.

I told the firefighters they were being paid to answer fire calls, not me, and why were they waking me up for that kind of crap anyway? What did they want me to do, prescribe some KY jelly to the old geezer so the Major wouldn't light some kind of friction fire? I didn't take even a moment to consider the underlying pathologies, to ask the "what if" question, like, what if there's a day when pulling the fire alarm isn't enough, and a bunch of old people die in their beds because the Major lights up the toilet paper in the bathroom? I thought about that for weeks, waiting to read about the fire. I probably should have sent him upstairs to see the pro shrinks – at least then it wouldn't be on my conscience if anything happened.

Maybe, just maybe, if I cared more about the "underlying pathologies," I would have spotted Miller earlier, right? I'm rambling – I know it, but it's hard not to ramble when you're just trying to do the best you can, and all you really want to do is sleep. Ever fall asleep while you're driving? That's what it's like – you're so tired that you can feel your eyelids dropping, even though you know exactly how dangerous it is. Your head messes you up – just for a second, your eyelids say, just for a second. Coming back from a day in the country, everyone a little sunburned and sleepy, and the next thing you know you're in a hospital bed and you're alone, everyone else having died in the emergency room hallway or before the firefighters could even cut them out of my SUV.

Sorry. I'm just sorry. So I work harder, and carry crosses like this guy.

I was fading right there in the room with Miller, fading, though he seemed like a real dangerous guy to be ignoring, even for a moment. He was telling me about his apartment, about how it was bugged, about how his knees were shot from driving and he lived above a stereo shop.

"That's what I did, see, is I took all the styrofoam from the empty boxes, just the flat sheets from in front of the screens, and I put that down all over the apartment floors, see, because it lessens the impact. Also the noise." He was talking faster, kind of gabbling, and I was still collecting symptoms, or at least keeping track of them, checking them off as he went. Nothing I could cure in this guy, so I wanted to be rid of him – although the styrofoam, that seemed like a good idea.

Impatience – that was a big problem with me. If you can't fix 'em right away, make the diagnosis and shift 'em upstairs. That's one reason I work well in emergency – you keep them moving, and only do the magic that you're sure you can deliver.

I always thought my hands were magic – that's the kicker, really. I'd be sewing someone up – real fine work, a cut over an eyebrow or somewhere a scar would show real easily, and it would be as if I was standing back and my hands were doing the work all by themselves. Fine work, too, not the slap-dash needlepoint that some doctors call stitches – if it was someone I ran into again later, I'd always keep an eye out, to see if the scar was as fine as I expected it to be.

Not a lot of people like to work the emergency room shifts. The hours are a killer for family life, for one, and then there's the chance of doing something wrong: get someone on the table with their chest filling up with blood, a crushing chest injury like hitting the dashboard when you're speeding along at 100, and you've got to get a tube in there and drain things before the lungs collapse.

But the emergency room is to medicine like slaughtering cattle is to working in a French restaurant – the emergency room is fast, messy medicine, and you're pushing a tube in between someone's ribs and hoping you don't accidentally do more damage in there.

It's got to be done, and quickly. Otherwise somebody's wife just dies there in the hallway while her husband's unconscious and can't tell the other doctors what they should be doing. It's best guesses, and heaven help you if you guess wrong, because even if the families never figure out what you did wrong, you know it. I always figured that if anything happened, I'd be able to do something about it – I never figured I'd be a patient, too, the kind who wakes up three days after an accident and can only remember what they tell him about it. Flail chest – all the ribs broken on one side – it must hurt like hell, but I know what to do about it, damn it, I know exactly how to put in the drain, and do it right away to lessen the stress on the lungs. That way, everything won't just shut down while she's out there lying on a gurney, waiting for somebody to get around to wheeling her down to x-ray. Enough blood inside the chest wall and the lungs collapse, away she goes, unable to even call out to me for help. I don't let it get that far, because I don't second-guess, waiting on x-ray time.

Miller was pissing me off. Maybe, I thought, maybe I'll tell him he needs a rectal exam just for spite, or order up some particularly nasty diagnostics, just to get even for all the time he's wasting – no, no, really, doctors don't do things like that, no matter what kind of jerk you are.

And then I realize he's stopped talking, and he's just sitting there staring at me, and he has to realize that I'm not paying attention at all. And that's just about the worst thing I could do, because it's feeding the pathology – the guy already thinks doctors are the enemy, unwilling to listen, and I'm proving the point. And it's not even because I don't care. It's because I'm so damned tired that my eyes are starting to cross, and even I know that I'm a danger to patients when I'm like this.

And now I'm a danger to myself as well. Miller has picked up the knife.

The strange thing is, the only thing I can think is that I'm going to get stabbed because a trombone player wants to get a hard-on, and how fair is that?

No one from the floor had been in to see if everything was all right – sooner or later, a nurse would have to poke her head in to tell me we had a cardiac on the way – Friday night, there's always one or two, but it was near shift-change and they were probably all finishing up their paperwork.

"You should just tell him to stop," Miller says, digging under his fingernails now with the tip of the knife. "Haven't tried that, have you?"

"What?" I wasn't sure what he was talking about.

"The trombone player," he said.

I hadn't told him a thing about the trombone player.

"You could ask him to stop. That is, if he's really there at all."

I lost my temper then, and banged my hand flat and hard on the countertop, the noise loud enough to startle even me.

"What the hell do you know about my life, buddy?" I shouted at him. "And what's it matter anyway? I've got better things to be doing than dealing with you."

"I know you're pretty out there, doc. I know you're wound right up. And I don't know if you're in any shape to be treating patients."

I just stared at him. "Is that your diagnosis?" I said coldly.

"I don't know," he said. "You're the doc. At least I know what's going on with me. How about you?"

He grabbed his clothes with one hand, slouched down from the table, and touched me under the ear with the tip of the knife.

"I think maybe you're not a blue after all."

Then he walked out the door of the examining room and headed down the hall. I heard him whistling in the hallway, whistling *Blue Moon*, so I must have said something about my trombone neighbour, but I don't remember when or what.

"Without a dream in my heart,
Without a love of my own…"

I sent Scott after him, the biggest orderly we have, and Scott likes to tussle. When he's off shift with us, he works downtown as a bouncer, and I've seen his hands after some weekends, the knuckles ripped up and scabbed over. I told Scott that Miller had a knife, told him to get the cops. I felt under my ear, but there wasn't any bleeding.

When Scott came back, he just shook his head. There had been a trail of footprints in the fresh snow, he thought, but only until he'd reached a busier street.

"Sorry, doc," he said. I noticed Scott's hair was full of loose and perfect snowflakes. "No sign of him."

No sign at all.

Dealing with Determinism

HELEN SAID SHE WOULDN'T GO — AND SHE didn't.

"No way," she said, not even looking up from her book. "It's just a bunch of drunks I don't know, and all their cigarette smoke and noise. I can't think of a worse way to spend an evening." She was in their bedroom, a blanket over her legs, knees drawn up into a small but stubborn mountain range.

"I've got to go," Kevin said, standing at the foot of the bed. "It's the Christmas party. I'm expected."

"You're expected? It's your office. Go ahead then. It doesn't mean I'm expected."

"Fine."

It was, he thought, an argument they used to find time to have. But now they just walked away, positions entrenched. They had reached a point, Kevin thought, where arguments were over before they began. It was the flash point that wasn't — it was, he thought, surrendering, giving up, letting go.

Outside, there was wet snow already. The spruce trees were heavy with it, and there was enough down on the road that the occasional cars left tire tracks that lasted only moments before they started to fill in. Pulling out of the driveway, before the tires bit down to the pavement, Kevin stepped on the gas and the back end of the truck gave a sudden shuddering lurch to one side, and for one small moment, he thought about backing up and just pulling back into the driveway. But the thought made him set his jaw, and he drove away.

Later, it would occur to him that somehow it was all her fault, just because she wouldn't go, that it would have been different if she had. And what an easy way out that was: it was his first excuse.

But he had others.

"There aren't good guys or bad guys," he liked to say afterwards to anyone willing to listen to him talk about it. "Nothing is as simple as that. Nothing is black and white." Just saying it wasn't his fault, that there were other things involved, that none of it would have happened if things had been going better between them.

"You don't just go out and sleep with someone else," he'd say, defensively, as if it were some kind of legitimate explanation, as if it wasn't exactly what he had done.

Sure, he would think sometimes, sure it was sordid and tawdry and everything else. Thinking about the way a girl named Pat from customer service at the office had put her hand on his leg under the table, and that it wasn't an accident, and that her hand had moved slowly up his thigh while he had tried to keep talking, his mind spinning while his body responded urgently to her touch. Pat Connolly, small and blond, packed into a short black formal dress: he had seen her coming up the stairs to the second floor of the bar, Pat and Denise Mouland and the new girl from the front counter, the quiet, skinny one with the big, hollow eyes. Kevin couldn't remember her name.

The group had settled onto the bench on Kevin's side of the table, with Pat pushing down against him because there wasn't quite enough room.

It could have been innocent enough at first, he reasoned, because they had all been laughing, and her hand fell on his shoulder first. Collegial, even though her hand felt charged against his back. They all had free drink tickets, numbered tickets unwound from the same big red coil, and the table – a long pine table with heavy benches on both sides – was covered with empty beer bottles by then. The bar was on two levels, and downstairs half the office was dancing on the small dance floor, laughing as they picked out '70s music to dance to – right then, Dire Straits and the Sultans of Swing. Kevin could see that all together, they virtually filled the Rabbit's Foot, the small, dark bar the company had rented for the evening – that had been an office joke for weeks, he remembered, who was "going to get lucky at the Rabbit's Foot."

It was a better spread than some years: this time, big trays of broccoli and celery and carrots with sour cream dip, cold cuts and finger food – a small crowd developed every time another tray of hot wings was brought out.

Everyone was talking at once, and as it got louder and louder, Kevin felt as if he could disappear into the sound, drown in it, as if it would fill the room and overflow.

Except for her hand on his leg, and the fire that seemed to be burning in his thigh, and in two spots he could feel glowing high on his cheekbones. He found it hard to comprehend that she would even be interested in him; a mid-level newspaper manager with a paunch just starting to swell over his belt, a man who stood in the shower every morning, inspected the handfuls of shampoo foam and rinsed his hands of the bunches of loose hair that departed with every wash.

The conversation at the table had deteriorated into pocket philosophy, into the fuzzy world of beer debate. The argument was a simple one: whether people choose their own direction, or whether events and upbringing make the choice for them.

"In the end, it's your choice," an editor named Pinsent was arguing, yelling over the rest of the room. "Whatever you do, you do."

Kevin shook his head firmly. "You don't always get to pick," he said.

And then he was downstairs in a hallway near the coats, no cognitive decision about it, and her skirt was rucked up over her hips, his hands on her ass. Nothing subtle about that. The bar around them was like an exhaled, smoky breath, and all the coats smelled like wool from the heavy wet snow outside. Remembering it later, critical pieces seemed to be missing: he could remember the exquisite feeling of her fingers on his arm, but he could not remember walking down the stairs to the coats.

Sometimes, he would decide that the rest of it had been a horrible mistake — and then, mere seconds later, that none of it was a mistake at all. One thing he thought he knew for sure was that, if the evening had all been cued up again like an unrolling spool of film, everything would have happened in exactly the same order — with exactly the same result. Gears will turn true, and clocks will tick ever forwards. And there's not a minute that can ever change the length of its period.

Then Julie and David came down the hall, leaving the party — Julie from accounting, and her boyfriend David, who had worked for a few years in the front office. They were finding their coats, pulling them down from the hangers sharply so that the wooden hangers rattled back against the wall. Both of them studiously keeping their eyes high, fixing their stares above Kevin's flushed face, avoiding both his eyes and the sight of Pat still standing tight against him.

"Leaving already?" Kevin asked. Julie was tall and slim, her mouth pursed small. She was, Kevin thought, too young to have fashioned her face into such a deliberate knot of disapproval.

"Yes," she said, and Kevin had never heard a single word said so coldly.

At the same time, having the couple come down the hall to the coatroom was an easy break – nothing had really happened yet, Kevin thought, nothing that couldn't be explained by too much beer. Because David and Julie had stopped – well, Kevin wasn't really sure what they had stopped, couldn't decide exactly what would have happened next.

It was a chance to get away, even if he wasn't looking to escape. There was just this thin warning in his head that if there was ever an opportunity to pull back, this was it, and that the chance would not come again. Decisions made of small moments that look like instant choices, but really aren't that at all, he thought. The decisions are made much earlier – it just isn't obvious when or how they are made.

Pat was fixing her lipstick and pulling her skirt back down over her hips, first one side, then the other.

"Give me a drive home, would ya?" she said, grabbing him by the wrist. He tried hard not to pull away, the sudden possessiveness in her grip unnerving him.

"No, I can't," he said, the possibilities and dangers whirling through his head all at the same time.

And then he did anyway.

While he drove, Kevin tried to work it out rationally: he tried to think about chaos theory, wanted to consider just plain inescapable original sin. But the words rattled around in his head, empty, meaningless. The snow battering against the windshield, for a moment an image of Helen sleeping with the book face down on the blanket, the whirling feeling you get when you dance too fast… Then Pat's hand on his thigh again. Kevin putting on the turn signal, pulling the truck off the side of the road into deeper snow. Philosophy meaning very little in the instant.

The gearshift was in the way and they wrestled for a few moments with stubborn and uncooperative clothing: later he remembered seeing, over his shoulder her bare foot on the dashboard in the orange of the streetlight. Jarring, moving memories – cars flicking by on the road, the snow starting to pile up on the glass with fat wet flakes, Pat's breathing. And the disconcerting feeling that he was somehow watching everything from a distance, an observer, rather than a participant.

They didn't speak while they drove the last few blocks to Pat's driveway: a small suburban house, her apartment in the basement with only a few windows that could even catch light. The two windows on the front were lit yellow from the lights inside, but the snow was filling the windows in.

"Want to come in?" Pat asked.

"No," Kevin said quietly. "I don't think so. But thanks."

"All right then. That was nice," Pat said, out of the truck quickly and slamming the door, heading up towards the house. She waved over her shoulder without looking back. Kevin put the truck in reverse, and backed away.

Driving through the snow, the flakes catching in the headlights and then rushing eagerly towards the front of the truck, the evening came back to him in a visceral rush that he could feel right through the centre of his body. He could still taste the smoke on Pat's lips, still feel the fluid curve of her hips arcing against his own. It felt to him that he had been painted, all over, with a special sort of paint that you couldn't help but see. And he tried to look back and convince himself that it had been wrong – but it was a difficult equation to work through, without coming up with exactly the same answer, the same action.

No matter how he put it together, he ended up in the same place, feeling her fingers spread and gripping his back – knowing that he shouldn't have done it, but that he would have done it again, without a moment's extra thought.

You get what you build, he thought, and I've built this. Watching the snowflakes fall, each one's staggering tumble explainable, even if the calculation is so incredibly complex as to render it unprovable.

He pulled into his own driveway, turned off the headlights and the engine, and sat there. Listening to the engine tick as it cooled, watching the snowflakes at first melting on the windshield, and then starting their slushy climb up the glass.

Inside, in bed, Helen is sleeping, Kevin thought. She's sleeping, and for her, absolutely nothing has changed. The world is still spinning true, and will stay that way, axis near to vertical, for hours, maybe even for days. He walked up from the truck, turned the key in the lock slowly, keenly aware of the wobble that his world had developed.

He walked around the dark kitchen, picking things up and putting them back down again. No real order to his choices: a pepper mill, a wooden spoon, the hem of a dishcloth hanging from the handle of the oven. Walking through the living room, still touching things as if trying to convince himself that they, at least, were solid and familiar. And they were familiar: even though he felt as if they should all be changed under his touch, every single thing was where it should be. Then he climbed the stairs, his hand loose on the railing.

He could hear Helen breathing in the darkened room, steady, long breaths that ended in a half-snore he had always loved teasing her about. The light from outside, leaking from the edges of the curtains, lit up pieces of the room: a bed table here, the edge of the comforter at the foot of the bed.

For a moment, he wasn't sure what to do next. He could feel his hand tight around the key ring in his pants' pocket, the truck key large and sharp-edged and ready.

Instead, he undid his belt, took off his pants and shirt, and, naked, slid into bed, still distracted by the reality that the sheets felt exactly the way they had when he had gotten up that morning.

Then, almost of its own accord, his right hand reached for her, cupping the dome of her right shoulder. She was sleeping on her left side, her back to him.

Helen murmured in her sleep, and nestled her back in against his stomach, against his groin.

He wanted to say wait, this is not what I thought … but the thought was a fleeting one. She was naked and warm, and Helen. He felt himself getting aroused, and at the same time, horrified.

She rolled onto her stomach, and arched towards him again, both familiar and eager.

He suddenly realized, his hand resting flat on the middle of her back, the skin there soft and sleeping-warm, that he was trying to say with his body what he couldn't say out loud. He thought of it as a warning, like yelling for help without ever speaking – and also, strangely, an attempt to make things right again.

Desperate and determined, trying to prove he was exactly the person he always had been, yet frantic about whether or not he would be able to pull it off. It was, in the end, a rivetting combination. When it was over, he shuddered violently and fell back against the bed.

For a moment, the room was almost silent, only the sound of their competing breathing in the dark.

Then, fully awake, Helen finally spoke. Even, slow words, each one shaped carefully, each one dropped like a pebble.

"Now," pulling the sheet back up over her breasts, "what exactly is it that you're trying to tell me?"

Bowling Night

H E TOOK THE BOWLING BALL, AND LET THE car burn.

His hand was already sweaty around the handle of the bag. The ditch beside the road was full of clover and bees. Long, even rows of apple trees ran down the hill, the fruit heavy and reddening and pulling the branches down, and behind him, his car wasn't only smoking. It was well alight now, the windows gone, red-orange flames boiling out and the oily black smoke standing straight up in the sky in an ever-widening column.

Ray had felt, more than heard, the windows blow out, scattering safety-glass diamonds into the grown-over road gravel and out onto the hot, late-August road. He hadn't looked back as the sound rolled over him, hadn't turned around once, just kept walking awkwardly down the long incline towards New Minas, shifting the bag from one hand to the other every hundred feet or so. He wasn't used to walking any more, just like he wasn't used to putting on a coat in the depths of winter because the car was next to the house, his keys familiar in his hand. Walking along the side of the highway, he could feel his thighs rubbing together with each step, and his legs already felt damp and sweaty inside his jeans.

The tires had lit by then, and each one exploded with a muffled thump. When the police came and ran the burned, ridged numbers of the licence plate through their computer, it told them that the registered owner was Ray Hennessey, General Delivery, Gaspereaux, Nova Scotia. And Ray was far away already, walking. As he walked, he looked at the long runs of escaped foxglove and lupin running down below the shoulder of the road, and he wondered how long it had been since he had actually smelled the full, sweet scent that blew off the flowers.

It had all started with a fight with Jenine – everything started with a fight now. Or ended with one. And it was almost impossible to reconcile this Jenine with that other Jenine, the Jenine who had been so quiet, sitting with a small knot of her friends in the club at Evangeline Beach.

Then, the club had been a regular summer hangout, and teenagers had driven from Kentville and New Minas, from Windsor and Hantsport and Wolfville, to dances in the close, muggy airless club – thick with the smell of chewing gum and beer and sweaty bodies – the only break from the heat coming when the piled-cloud thunderstorms rolled up the length of the valley from Digby and brought a short few hours of respite. Then, the curtains beside the open windows would breathe in and out with the short, sharp breaths of cool, post-rain air.

Now, what had been the long, open dance floor was crowded with pinball machines and video games, and there was a tired shop counter where you could buy charcoal and potato chips, hotdog buns and almost-cold soft drinks. The building sagged, broken-backed at some point along its sills, settling into the contour of the ground. A desultory and thinly-attended mini-golf course sat by the back door, eighteen holes dressed in frayed green outdoor carpet. Battered putters lay forgotten under a dusty grey layer, a thin skin of oxidation from the salt air. Around the back, a small forest of camper-trailers had grown up, permanent residents who parked their campers high on cinder blocks, planted gardens and built brick barbecues. They came out every weekend to shout greetings to the same familiar neighbours. Not a journey, just a simple change of backdrop for actors in the same play.

The high brown tides of Minas Basin were chewing away at the promontory where the club sat, and each year, the owners had truckloads of boulders and the remains of road work dumped there to hold back the sea – flat black oozing plates of asphalt, squares of concrete sidewalks, busted-up pieces of curbs and gutters. But the winter storms chewed all of that away, sucking the pavement slabs out into the mud and scattering them deep in the bay.

There had been, for years, a long point of land there, stretching above the ruler-flat beach. On hot nights, when ice melted in your glass faster than you could drink, you could stand under a string of coloured lights at the end of the point and look out over the dark bay – wherever the tide was, whether you were looking over bare mud flats and shingle beach or over the flat, waveless surface of the bay, it gave the same inky black impression: it was a necessary opposite, the negative to the flat silver of the day. The red-brown sandstone was eaten away in layers on the outcrop, each thin sliver, each ragged step in the stone a collection of hardened centuries melting away.

When the moon rose full over the long ridge of Blomidon to the south, you could lean on the railing and watch the swifts and swallows scoop up swamp mosquitoes and midges just as the last of the light failed.

He had met Jenine out there. She had been standing near the rail, waving a hand uselessly at the cloud of insects. The swallows wheeled in, dark shapes with their wings folded flat against their bodies like darts, gathering flies from just above their heads.

And they were awkward together then, an awkwardness that would punctuate their relationship until it finally became a constant, barely-recognized background note.

He was on a road crew that summer, holding a sign for ten hours a day, and his skin was tanned to the colour of leather, at least to the line marked by the sleeves and collar of his T-shirt. Later, seeing himself in the mirror in the half-light of the bedroom, Ray would think that it looked as if he was always wearing a white T-shirt, the difference in colour between his arms and shoulders so abrupt that he could have been parts of two different people awkwardly joined above the elbow and at the neck. It made him feel that taking off his clothes was particularly revealing, and that Jenine was the only person who ever really saw him.

Eventually, they had a loose, comfortable offhandedness that suited them both well; they walked in the evenings on the long dykes that held back the Bay of Fundy from the low fields behind, tracing the spine of the dykes when the evening was calm, taking the gravel road below the dykes when there was wind, watching the grasshoppers panic and careen away in long arcs from their footsteps. Sometimes, when they were walking along the top of the dyke, small touches of wind would run across the green wheat below, turning the heads of the wheat and leaving long silver fingerprints that vanished as the plants straightened up again when the wind moved away.

And even the small house in Gaspereaux didn't change that ease, a tiny house, built for generations of smaller people, with low ceilings and shallow closets and walls that the wind seemed to whisper right through. In the winter, broad feathers of frost spread across the windows, and some mornings the outdoors looked as if you were staring at the day through the warble of bottle glass. The drafts spun around their ankles and the only warmth was deep in bed.

They got the car then, so that they could drive into Wolfville for groceries, a big, flat-nosed boat of a car, a gold and white LeMans, rusting along the bottoms of the doors but with a great wide bench of a seat, a long car loose in the turns, especially when the road was icy. It drank gasoline by the gallon and sometimes smoked, but when they were driving, Jenine would unclasp her seatbelt and move over close to him, their legs touching, and put her hand on the inside of his thigh. With the windows rolled up and the radio on, they drove folded into each other, protected from the world outside.

It became a difficult car when the children were born – the doors heavy and long, making it hard to maneuver two little boys into their backseat car seats – but it was what they had, so it was as simple as that.

At first, it was enough – making do was enough, now that he was driving dump truck instead of just holding signs, and the cheques were better, the work more steady, even if there was a span in the early spring when the plowing was finished, the roadwork hadn't started and money was tight.

But everything he thought couldn't change, did.

Maybe, he thought, it was the children, turning Jenine almost imperceptibly at first, bending the compass away from north like a magnet set too close. And it wasn't that he didn't love both of them – he did desperately, breathlessly at times, especially when they lay sleeping, their arms soft against the sheets in the half-light. But Jenine loved them more — Ray would admit that to himself sometimes, quietly, like when he caught her putting their pyjamas in the wash, holding the small shirts to her face as if trying desperately to find their scent deep in the flannelette. And it occurred to him that she had only so much love to share, and that his portion was now necessarily smaller.

But he hadn't changed, he thought. He hadn't.

Jenine had learned a bitter smile, he noticed, a fixed and hard smile he had never seen before.

It was like driving at night, like being forced down the tunnel of your headlights, able to see what was coming but unable to avoid smashing into it. Like falling, but with the benefit of knowing exactly where the fall was leading, and knowing at the same time that he was powerless to change any of it.

"You could at least try for the foreman's job," she said, her back to him while she stood at the sink, the words bouncing back off the window glass. "You could try, if you had any initiative at all."

A vindictive tone in her voice, a brassy satisfaction like she was daring him to say something else. And he would try to fight back — he could have told her the job was already Mike's, because Mike was dating the owner's daughter — but his heart wasn't in it. And somehow that was even worse.

An argument would build between them like a storm rolling down the valley, but before it burst into the open, he would be distracted by a hard-shelled flying bug tapping the kitchen light bulb, or the awk-

ward flutter of the curtains caused by someone opening a door somewhere else in the house.

He would lose his train of thought and, that thread
lost, he would find himself unable to argue any more.

And Ray began to notice things that he had never
seen before; how the jagged-edge alder leaves on the
bank behind the house were so much darker, their
green much duller, than the other trees. How the
catkins on those same alders stayed hard and green,
virtually until the single day when they all at once
turned brown and broke open, scattering the near-
invisible seeds to the wind. How the fairy-ring mush-
rooms – light brown with torn, embattled, soft-
rotting black edges – formed a ragged circle in the
same place in the yard, every year, acting out the
organic memory of a tree he had long ago forgotten.

How the baking cherries turned colour from
green to flesh, and then the dark green leaves were
punctuated all over with bright red round dots.

The months clicked over like numbers on the
odometer, steadily marching, white on black.

And then, when the fights started, the fights he
could never win because he didn't even know how to
properly begin, he would just pick up the bowling
ball and leave, heading for New Minas, leaving the
front door open on the white house and hearing the
shouted words chasing him down the driveway –
"Tell me what you're thinking. Just say what it is
you're thinking" – and he'd wonder who was yelling
as he yanked the shift into reverse and backed down
the drive.

He was, by now, a big man, used to greasy spoon lunches and eating on the fly, and when he moved quickly, sweat would sprout in unexpected places. But at the bowling lanes on Wednesdays, he had a strange poise. He held the ball high and moved to the line with small steps, almost mincing, something close to a heavy man's ballet while his stomach preceded him. And his arm would whip back and then flow forwards in one motion, and he would release the ball in a spinning shallow curve, angling towards the ten-pin from a direction it never seemed to expect.

Holiday Lanes in New Minas had just ten lanes, ten pins each, one hundred soldiers standing in formation. It was small and noisy and battered, but strangely self-contained, a whole small world of clatter and order. Knock all the pins down, and magically their formation would reappear.

Ray was on a team with three of the other dump drivers, and they hadn't ever won the league trophy, but they often came close.

And the other drivers would talk about teen conquests, spectacular wrecks, and whether John Andrews had really cracked Helen Devries on a picnic table at the beach on prom night, the way he always boasted he had – twenty years had passed but it was still the subject of great debate – and Ray would sit quietly, turning the big ball in his hands, waiting for his turn.

He was the best player on the team, his aim constant, his score always high, and Ray sometimes felt as if he could simply will the ball to curve, so sharply did it bite against the slick lane and turn for the headpin. Then, his turn over, he'd sit again, feeling the ball under his hands as smooth as glass.

They'd drink too many beers to drive, and then drive anyway, counting on their experience and occasionally veering wildly onto the shoulder, throwing gravel. And when the cops saw them, the police would pull their cruisers into the first available driveway, turn around, and drive the other way.

When they ripped up the sidewalks in Wolfville that summer, Ray's truck — a big red tandem-wheeled dump with jake brakes and a persistent, constant exhaust leak into the cab that left his tongue oily with diesel smoke at the end of each day — was one of the dump trucks that hauled the used gravel and broken pavement out to Evangeline Beach, dumping it down the long slope in front of the threatened club. And even Ray could see that it was a war they were losing, could see it more clearly with each load. He could see that the strong tides started moving the heaviest of the pavement squares in only a few days, the fine silty mud and sand shifting and undercutting the slabs, and the tide worrying the cliff like a dog at a dead rabbit. It was obvious that the club had only a few more winters. If that.

At the end of each day he'd wait in Wolfville where they parked the trucks in sight of the night watchman, a reedy man who smoked constantly, his cigarette a small scarlet lighthouse signalling warning amid the shoals of a craggy and deeply lined face. And every day, Ray's head pounded from the exhaust and the heat, from the dust and the blatting roar of the downhill brakes, and he'd wait until Jenine picked him up to angrily drive him over the hill to home.

By August, the pile in front of the club was broad and fanning out, but every morning, Ray could see another few pavement slabs that had skimmed away down the flat beach on the receding tongue of the tide.

When the sidewalks were done, they took down DeWolfe's apple warehouse, because the trains had stopped and the apples went away by truck as soon as they were picked. They took the roof down first and saved the big beams, but when the roof was gone, the company brought in a crane with a wrecking ball and smashed the high walls down in a single afternoon, because it was the only safe thing to do. The collapsing walls raised clouds of dust that caught in Ray's nose. An excavator filled his truck, and Ray drove the scraps of warehouse away.

They took down every single thing except the building's chimney, three storeys high and unused for years, and they only kept that because, on summer evenings, hundreds of chimney swifts would return at dusk and boil backwards down the chimney like a huge cloud of smoke travelling in reverse.

Ray painted the house that year with another coat of white paint, old oil paint from the shed, heavy and glutinous and pulling back at the brush with almost as much force as he could muster to pull it forward. And one Wednesday evening, when he had finished hating window trim about as much as he believed he could hate any single thing, he pounded the paint cans shut in the dark and slab-sided shed, knowing at the same time that he would have to paint it all again the next summer.

And perhaps the fight started because he had gotten so much trim paint on the glass. It didn't matter. Ray forgot almost everything about the fight quickly, distracted by a bumblebee that had found its way into the kitchen, flying slowly and angrily and butting its head against the windowpanes, unable to find its way out. He could see the bristly yellow-and-black, the fat summer pods of pollen on the bee's front legs like saddlebags, the way the bee used its feet to scrabble futilely against the glass for a few moments after every single collision. He remembered standing by the window, pushing the window up and letting the bee out, watching the gooey strands of white paint stretching and breaking between the window and the sill. He remembered the shape of the door, the feel of the doorknob in his hand. But he couldn't remember Jenine's face or even the sound of her voice.

Then he was in the car, driving on the highway. The engine warning light came on, orange, and then the red oil light, but Ray drove without moving his head, his face planed calm and staring, the radio talking loosely to someone else, turned too low to be heard. The engine started knocking hard as the car climbed the first long ridge of the highway, crossing the big iron bridge over the Gasperaux. The big bridge the highways department would sandblast clean and repaint every summer, and every year, the fat-knuckled boils of rust would reappear by spring.

At the top of the hill, the dials on the dashboard went wild, and the car stopped, lurching once onto the shoulder, and smoke started to curl out from under the hood. He sat there watching, futilely turning the key over and over again. Nothing. In the middle of the hood, the paint started to blister and peel back all by itself, leaving a widening, blackening circle, more smoke coming out from the edges of the hood all the time. He sat, listening to hisses and crackles as the radio stopped, and thin wisps of smoke rose from around his feet. Then he took the key out of the ignition, lifted his bowling ball off the seat, locked the doors, and started walking away down the long inclined plane of the Five-Mile Hill towards New Minas. Soon, there were sirens coming up from Wolfville, but he kept walking.

A firefighter standing next to the burning car saw Hennessey just before he disappeared from sight, just before his body sank below the hill and his head and neck were wobbly from the heat-shimmer off the pavement. And the firefighter pointed him out to the police – by then only the dome of Ray's head and his white shirt visible, the distance robbing him of arms – while the big pump on the fire engine was still thrumming and the water hitting the LeMans made the hot metal ping and snap. The fill-line to the gas tank had burned off, and a large puddle of gasoline was burning on the pavement.

The police car crept up behind Ray slowly, its right-side tires crackling on the gravel shoulder, but he still didn't turn around.

Not until a policeman touched him gently on the shoulder.

Then Ray swung the bowling ball desperately in its handled bag, and another, more cautious policeman edged in behind him and broke the bone at the point of Ray's elbow with a sharp rap of his nightstick, a motion as easy and gentle as a caress, the practiced, slow motion of a cook breaking the first egg on the edge of a pan.

And even after Ray dropped the bowling ball, it took four policemen to put him in the back of their car. Down in the ditch, the bees took turns marching into the garish funnels of the foxgloves, and the clover bobbed and nodded its silent approval.

The Latitude of Walls

"SHE'S SCREAMING."

"She always screams."

It was cotton-dark on the stairs, cotton-dark and gripping, the kind of dark that fills corners, fills the corners and rests there, waiting.

And the sound of the screaming seeped through the wall, muffled like wool, shadowed and thin, the edges planed, the tops and bottoms all lost. Without tympani or piccolo, but screaming nonetheless. Words indistinct, but tone definite.

Cold on the stairs, the draft falling off the big window halfway up, air falling down between the gaps in the stair treads, running away into cracks in the floor, meeting crumbs and dust and spiders, toppling into the crawl space beneath. And even after the scream stopped, he could hear it, echoing, thin and whispered, known, tattooed as much as remembered. It was the sort of sound, the kind of harmonic that sets up its own place, that rings in a way that lets it hang in memory like a finger, held chin-high and in front of you, pointing outwards. The kind of sound that, once heard, is never forgotten. And the night pressed too close, the wind up outside and shaking. The night gloved and fingered and touching, the trees rattling branches like bare finger bones. Outside, a fine-footed cat walking tightrope, one careful foot in front of another, intent and distant, lone-walking, fur-sleeking, far away and into the garbage behind the fence. And then, after a moment, the screaming again, low, guttural and feral.

"I'm telling you, she's screaming," Kevin Hennessey said. He was only new there, recently separated from his wife, living in a friend's narrow house like a transient in an alley, caught in between so tightly that he could reach out and touch the walls that hemmed him in. New enough that he could still feel the shape and style of his previous life around him like furniture, placed and unmoving, feet settled into the carpet, making dimples.

He had always expected that he would stay: leaving home had seemed like a long, virtually impossible hill, something that maybe could be climbed, but only if you could ever find the energy. It was always there, always something just on the edge of the possible as the desperation built, until one day he found himself wildly throwing shirts and underwear into a duffel bag.

By then, neither he nor his wife were sleeping more than three hours a night, the rest of the darkness torn apart with tears and quiet, bitter fights. Exhaustion took as much of a toll as anything else: days were a hopeless tangle of confusion and the blank stare left over from sleeplessness. Leaving became necessity; the rest of his world had been out of his control, taken over by the Coriolis effect, spinning quick and clockwise, straight down the drain. Sometimes, that's exactly what Kevin blamed it all on: Gustave-Gaspard Coriolis, the nineteenth-century scientist whose examination of Newton's laws of motion of bodies explained both cyclones and the spinning whirlpool disappearance of bathwater. Pull the plug, watch it all go, watch a fine and curling twister rise up from the drain, the whirlpool column in the water silver-sided in the light – fragile, and yet cruelly constant. Often, that was as close to a reason as he could find: that he had taken a wrong step, and physics had inevitably intervened. It was that, or accept a personal blame he didn't really understand, or – more to the point – wasn't willing to put his finger on.

And later, when he unpacked, Kevin found he had brought not one single pair of socks, and, paradoxically, every pair of underwear he owned.

"Screaming. That's what she does," Heather Doane said. Heather, who owned the house, who had lived there for years, who knew the unevenness of the walls like a knuckle tracing the plaster, feeling each dip and rise, the longitude and latitude of walls. Heather, who knew it already, who knew things before he did: she recognized all his symptoms, knew the line and the dip and the sudden sinking plunge. And every now and then, in the dark, still, painful evenings, she would tell him it was alright, that he was doing all right, as if leaving home had all the formal stages, the halting forwards-backwards steps, of Alcoholics Anonymous.

Sometimes when he shuddered with sobs, the few times he did cry in front of her, she would place two or three supporting fingers gently on the outside of his elbow. Knowing that the simple connection of touch was essential: knowing too that anything more than the slightest touch was a dangerous invitation at a dangerous time.

For Kevin, the house was all still deliciously foreign. He would wake at night in that strange fog of unease, the momentary bump and slip of not knowing, of trying to make sense of foreign surroundings lit with unfamiliar light – the oblong of the streetlight-lit window somehow always wrong, in the wrong place. The room, soft and unthreatening, yet turned on edge, sideways-shifted.

The cat, black and white and short-haired, heard the screaming and didn't flinch, hardly paused, step-stepping carefully, more intent on each paw-lifting, paw-settling step than on the fugitive noises of neighbours.

Kevin, on the stairs, stopping. "Is she in trouble?"

"No."

"Why, then?'

"Because he left."

It was explanation set as punctuation – just the naked why. But Heather was sometimes like that: an explanation was unnecessary, as long as the outcome was clear. Eventually he learned more: that the neighbour was Mrs. Bird, that she had two cats, that Mr. Bird had left for work one evening like he always had, a night watchman prowling the periphery of an old-age home, alone with his thoughts and the buttonless night. Nothing to suggest he wouldn't be back in the morning, like always, sitting in his kitchen in his sleeveless undershirt, drinking one more cup of milky sweet tea. Heather said his face hung on his skull as if it had come unpressed, that it drooped away from the muscles beneath, and that every day he was there, waiting for the clock to count down to bed.

Except, one day, he wasn't. As easy and as unlikely as that. From the door of Heather's laundry room, looking across to the Birds' kitchen, Kevin could imagine a cup of tea, steaming, waiting. It was five years ago, Heather told him eventually, and still Mrs. Bird was keening, still waiting for the front gate to open at his quiet touch.

And still Kevin was learning the shape of the house he was living in, the pattern of the place. Learning when the hot water would fail two full inches before the bath was full. Already he knew that the rooms weren't square, although sometimes the variation was only slight: looking at the ceiling of the living room, it was possible to see that the back of the room was narrower than the front by a few inches. In other rooms, the unevenness was more pronounced, all the result of a house built to fit a space between its neighbours, on an oblong and long-used lot.

At night, when Heather was out, Kevin would wander the house, picking things up, setting them down, wondering about the history behind glass bottles, the heavy, green, once-stoppered Superior Lemonade bottle on a window ledge in the bathroom, the flat, flask-like bottle whose only features were the words "S.A. CHEVALIER'S LIFE FOR THE HAIR." Candlesticks were silent about their provenance, but rested inside cupboards with a particular pride of place. Wineglasses, all different styles, were organized in rows without any particular discernible order. Shelves of paperback books, speaking of half-remembered university English courses, whispering of not having been moved in years. Photographs of smiling couples he did not know, a wedding picture of Heather's, turned face down now that her husband was gone, where, smooth-cheeked and literally radiant, she looked like no Heather he had ever met.

And somehow, it was as if he might be able to find Heather's whole life in there, locked up in code, if only some sort of Rosetta stone would make itself obvious in among the tablecloth runners, or deep in the pine cupboard where the casserole dishes hid. But there was no simple solution there – even though there were telling pieces, like the careful imprint of her lips in lipstick on a glass waiting to be washed, the overall pattern eluded him. Sometimes, he could feel it in the air in front of him, as fine as the smell of lemon peel. As fine as the thin, high trill of Mrs. Bird, once again her own private ambulance, driving through the narrow highways of her halls, rising, fading, rising again.

One day, through her window, as he was heading out Heather's gate, he saw her, saw Mrs. Bird, saw that she was, in fact, the thin, stick-like woman he had expected, the very way he might have drawn her in his imagination, except for the fact it seemed there was no way a woman that small could generate a sound that full. She just wasn't big enough to be a bell that could ring with such a depth of tone. He saw her peering through the window, not standing in the centre of the glass, but off to one side, peering from the corner as if she were an adjunct to her own living room. Her mouth was firmly closed, a thin, disapproving line, but still he could hear the sound, could hear it as clearly as if the tone were still hanging there in the air, existing all on its own.

And for a moment, he knew exquisitely and absolutely, not just the smell of the zest of lemons, but everything, even the sight of the nubbled yellow peel on the side turned away from him: he felt he could know her entire universe from the space around her, as if her life was captured in the china figurines along the mantel, the seven wooden balustrades he could see behind her, climbing up, as if her hopes and fears and desires were crystallized in that three-foot-by-two-foot glass rectangle, in what it held, and what it did not. How it had never changed, how she raged through it, her voice battering with the unanswered question of why, why this had not been enough.

When she looked away, quickly, it was as if he had looked too carefully, as if she was shamed by what he might have seen or by what he knew. As if she had misplaced something, as if she was embarrassed that she couldn't put her finger on just exactly where it had gone.

He met her outside, later, moving down the icy lane, walking carefully in small, pointed, fur-topped black boots, her face down, her words indistinct and muffled in the wool of her coat. He took it for "good morning." The words had come tumbling out, a low rush, and he had picked up only the tone of them, the way they were thrown out in one single exhalation, as if discarded into the air.

She was past him then, her shoulders hunched and impossibly narrow, as if she might turn sideways and vanish completely. Kevin was sure that she kept talking after she passed, that the words had continued spilling out, falling over themselves and scattering like salt under her feet, becoming their own sort of murmured security as she fled.

One night, the snow came, filtering fine through the trees at first, not touching the branches, sifting flakes caught only by the light. Thin snow threading down in lines, and then there was more, filling the spaces between. In the laneway, the flakes fell in careful, tipped sequence into angled drifts, leaning against the fence on one side of the lane, so that when Kevin stumbled home through the shin-high, powdery snow, his footprints did not so much fill in as create their own forgiving, erasing avalanches.

And there was a woman with him, holding his hand loosely, trailing like kite string back behind him, her own footsteps toppling in like afterthoughts behind her. Just someone he had met while Heather was working the hospital night shift, Heather working another Friday night call-in as the emergency room filled with the bruised, the shattered, the drunk.

It was something about the corner of the woman's mouth, that's what he would remember later, just something about the corner of her mouth, a small ironic fold that appeared when she smiled, that made the two of them come together in the cigarette smoke and the downtown dark. Eventually, that half-smile would be the only thing he would even be able to conjure up of her, the only piece he could gather from memory's scattered threads. But Mrs. Bird, Mrs. Bird he would never forget.

A twitch of the curtains, an instant of Mrs. Bird's profile, the black bead of one sharp, alert eye, and he was taken for a moment with the image of crows fighting in mid-air, the way one will fold its wings and fall, as if broken, to escape while the other – knowing – will almost immediately follow suit, jinking vertically. Cut and parry, an ease of movement when another's move is understood implicitly. The unexpected, yet always expected.

Then he was inside Heather's house. Inside, to that unfolding of hope, to that small perfect wonder of falling, helpless, and never fearing the fall.

The inside of her leg, right and yet wrong. Familiar, and yet strangely unfamiliar, patterned with fine thin hairs that he could not see, that his fingers barely felt. Tracing the delicate "y" of a vein along the back of her arm, from elbow to wrist, a line the like of which he had never touched before, fine and magic and halting strange. The feel of her breath, battering urgent against his neck, her fingers grasping in the hair on the back of his head. The complexity of it, the roundness, the fullness, thick like the fat humid air of a steam-room, so that it was an effort just to breathe.

Detail streaming in, filling up, overflowing to the point that he began to slide away, saw the room grey-ing, so that suddenly he needed to feel less, yet wanted to feel everything.

And was it from next door, chilling like the thin thread of a cold draft seeping in under a door? Or was it there in the room then, where everything lived in immediate, sharply lit snapshots - the futon flat and revealed, its beige cover folded back by their move-ments together, the sheets and blankets heaved into fabric's round, damp topography. The long orange rectangle of the streetlight cast out across the floor. A leg, lit from ankle to knee, the shadowed curve of a smile, that small, distinct pool at her throat that might fill with a puddle of water, if only a bath were deep enough.

And that brought more images, unbidden and unwelcome. Another bed, a narrow, too-steep staircase, picture frames that stared back at him. The road, framed in the front windows of the house that he had left.

What's that noise, he thought; that hollow noise in my head.

She's screaming again, he thought.

Keening distantly, but directly, too, like Mrs. Bird could look through walls.

He knew then what he hadn't. Suddenly, he knew how the gate swings silent, frictionless, on its hinge pins after someone leaves, how night's heavy breaths sometimes shake the house, how the snow sometimes falls abruptly, so that it just appears in the morning without ever being seen in the air. Knew the sinking feeling of being caught tight in the twisting spin, with Gustave-Gaspard Coriolis carefully calculating how short a time it would take for him to slide completely out of sight.

Mrs. Bird, screaming like she always screams, screaming for the lost.

Screaming a scream that Mr. Bird would never, ever hear. But Kevin did, and he could both feel his own hand on the gate, leaving, and imagine watching that same gate swing shut behind him, its latch clicking with a near-silent but final tap.

Beside him, sleep-heavy and warm, the woman shifted and turned on her side, languorous and long and welcoming – and there.

Lost, and found, and hopelessly lost again, Kevin clamped both hands over his mouth, trying to keep the sound from flying out.

Mapping

JOHN HENNESSEY STARTED THE MAP WITH A ditch, with one small spot that would, for anyone else, have been absolutely unremarkable.

It was just a ditch, dug out every five or six years by a department of transportation backhoe. It held a small pool of standing water after it rained, fireweed in summer, and a long stretch of meadow ran away behind it, fragrant with timothy grass and low tangles of wild strawberry.

It wasn't that the ditch was special, and she wasn't the first accident victim he had ever seen — just the first to leave a permanent mark. He saw her every time he passed.

Standing, arms outstretched, one hand open and the fingers of the other folded inwards. She was ankle deep in ditch water, with the blood running down to her shoulders.

"Am I cut bad?" she asked. "Am I cut bad?"

He could see bone winking white through her scalp, and the washed-sky blue of her eyes. The rest of her face was scarlet with blood, and lit bright by the headlights of his truck.

Next to her, a dark-blue car wedged nose-down in the ditch. The bank rose up behind her, high with browning summer thistle. The car had hit it straight on. There was a silver-white dimple outwards through the windshield, where her head had hit the glass.

The summer night was quiet, the air heavy, rain coming, and not one person along the road had come to their door at the sound. All the houses stood dark, their backs turned.

Her scalp was pulled back and split just at the hair-line, and the blood pulsed in rapid, shallow waves. He told her to stand still, to stay where she was, leaning against the open car door, that there would be more help in a minute. Her sweater had been blue. There were others in the ditch, someone he couldn't see, moaning, and the driver sitting on the shoulder of the road, crying.

Sirens then, still far away, the sound tumbling down the night valley toward Broad Cove. The valley was spruce on both sides, heavy green running up to flat meadow.

He had known he would be the first firefighter there, the accident right around the corner from his house. He had fumbled with his fire coat and the latex gloves.

But there wasn't much he could do, except watch the blood pour over his hands like tide running in across flat sand, as he tried to staunch it while she watched, unblinking. Until the ambulance came, and it was suddenly like a dream.

Back at the station, he saw that he had dried blood on the cuffs of his sweatshirt, and he looked at the rusty stains blankly, as if wondering where they could have come from.

The car had hit a patch of loose gravel, just as the driver had started to turn. There were four kids, all teenagers, and one had fractured his skull, just above the ear. But it was the girl that he remembered.

Everything was a second either way, he thought. It was all like that – it was just as simple as being caught in the middle of an intersection when someone had a stroke and hit you broadside. One small step away, always.

The engines on the fire trucks ticked as they cooled.

The other firefighters filled the trauma kit with new rubber gloves, brought blankets from the store-room for the rescue truck. They looked past him, watching the ceiling fans, then inspected their hands. In the kitchen, someone dropped a coffee cup in the steel sink and swore. Hennessey tried to keep his mouth shut at the fire hall; more and more, the others had a way of looking around him when he talked. And he, around them.

They had been solicitous when Jodean left, had talked to him more, standing close and saying they should go downtown, that he should get out and meet people. But the closer they tried to get, the more he felt pushed away. Every attempt, every strained word, only serving to underline the differences.

They didn't understand about Jodean, he thought; sometimes he didn't understand himself. Maybe distance between people, between lovers, grows in inches, inexorably, until one morning you open your eyes and suddenly see those unexpected miles, stretching out backwards forever, and you realize you don't have the energy, could never have the energy, to undo those inching, methodical steps that lead you away from each other.

Six years she had lived with him, before walking in the door one day and undoing it all with the finality of cloth tearing. He'd been out for much of the night, a March night when it seemed that cars were intent on doing crumpled, broken-backed gymnastics into ditches. The firefighters had already levered a middle-aged woman out of the upside-down wreckage of a Ford Fiesta, had cut the door off a dirt-smeared van, and Hennessey had held a drunken man's head while Gord Tucker tied him to a backboard, blood from a cut over the man's eye running over Hennessey's gloved fingers and down into the man's collar.

Hennessey had come home with his defences down, with his clothes dirty and his thoughts disordered and wandering – images flashing through his head like light bulbs turning on and off randomly: blood on the glove of one hand; the way the starred and cracked windshield caught the lights from the trucks; the green-glowing, reflective stripes that were all you could see of the other firefighters at the edge of the headlights. So it was an unfair fight, if you could call it a fight at all.

Because he didn't fight: at least, he didn't fight outside their rules of engagement. He thought about that later, about the things he should have said, about what he might have said, and really, he had thought about it then as well, the words full and round on his tongue, yet stuck there, unable to fall. And he found it strange how the rules that define a relationship could form almost imperceptibly, could frame and define the space within as precisely and rigidly as walls define the inside of a house. He could feel the argument – quiet, words barely spoken, pauses long and unbroken – growing dangerous, tilting wildly, yet he had been unable, utterly unable, to find a way to stop it.

Any of it.

Then the accident on the hill became the first single sharp point on a map in his head; that was the way he thought of it. It was simple geographic punctuation, hard and fixed and distinct; time and space spun around it like the heavens around the North Star. At first, it was that one spot on the hilltop road, a spot he would avoid driving by when he could. But then, others appeared. More and more, every week, effortlessly, the map spread and grew like lichen on granite, a web of dots with fine lines between them. Bit by bit, it began to intrude, uncomfortable, like an eyelash caught in his eye that he couldn't seem to find. Driving through the fire district started to feel like a half-remembered dance, filled with steps that only partially made sense to him.

Sometimes, when he passed a place where a car had left the road on ice, even in summer his vision would fill in from the edges with the white dazzle of fresh snow, until the road was reduced to twin wavering wheel marks that ended with a memory of torn brush and battered metal.

There was the place where the orange van had pitched end-over-end, racing without headlights in the dark, throwing mechanic's tools around inside like hard metal rain before they sprayed out the burst doors and scattered, all silver and red on the pavement under the flashing emergency lights.

And the spot where a car rolled off the road in slushy snow, stopping upside-down in a flooded ditch, and they had all gotten soaked feeling around under the cloudy water for the missing driver, trying to find her by touch in the murky grey-brown silt. They'd searched for fifteen minutes before a neighbour told them the woman was inside her house, trying to warm herself in the bath. They put a neck brace on her while she sat naked in the bathtub, shivering, and Hennessey couldn't help but feel like they were intruding, the three firefighters in their bulky yellow coats, dripping wet themselves and speaking in soft, clipped sentences devoid of verbs.

"Scissors."

"Tape."

"Blanket."

Or the house where a woman named Beth had fallen first asleep, and then unconscious, and quietly bled to death hours after dental surgery, a nurse five feet away and knitting, the television remote control in her lap. And they had yelled at the unconscious woman and pinched her arm while her jaw yawned loose, trying for any sign of life, and the noise rattled around all out of place in a country kitchen with dark wood cupboards and a dirty bread knife on the drainboard, its blade streaked with butter.

The paramedics had tried desperately to find a vein, any vein, but her eyes had rolled away into her head for good while they worked and scattered medical scraps – torn gloves, syringe packages, the useless IV tubing – around her on the floor and the television chattered happily. And it was unnerving how much the mess bothered him – how much it bothered him while she lay dead, flat on the floor, arms spread when the paramedics stopped.

Skin as white as eggshells, he would think when he had to drive past her house, skin as white as eggshells, and her back – when they rolled her sideways to put her on the stretcher – was already starting to blossom purple, what little blood she had left pooling under her alabaster skin. Trying to revive her, he had felt the warmth of her bare skin through the gloves, and the familiarity was unsettling.

New points on the map would come on him unbidden, like a cold breath of wind off the water, when he hardly expected it.

Driving past the foundation of an abandoned house, he remembered the fire that had burned there late at night, spattering his helmet with black specks of flaming roof tar. They searched the basement for drunken teenagers until a refrigerator – and then the chimney – crashed through the kitchen floor and joined them in the basement, where they were scrabbling, nearly trapped, among flaming mattresses, boxsprings and stacked, broken furniture.

Or the drunk-driving accident that had wrapped a car tight around a librarian, and they had cut and pried for over an hour while she alternately screamed and cried, and it was all he could do not to put down the tools, press his gloved hand over her mouth and hiss, "Shut up!"

It rang in his head: "Shut up! Shut up!" And he could feel his hands on his ears, the unfamiliarity of the latex pressed against his own skin, the strange touch halfway between antiseptic and intimate. And he could remember looking at Jodean, seeing her as the woman in the car, full of horror at his thoughts.

"Just shut up. Just stop. Stop."

But he had said nothing, watching the planes of her angry face, the way her cheekbones stood out, long lines slanting downwards, the way her eyes looked at his for only an instant before flicking away, unable to hold his gaze.

Still, he couldn't argue with Jodean when she said that things had changed, couldn't explain to her that what had been so simple before had been subtly altered. That when he reached out to touch the side of her face, she moved away with a practiced, almost studied ease.

It all seemed just beyond the edge of his reach, as if he were short one crucial piece of information, had arrived one careless moment too late.

And still the map grew. He added each event – sometimes new, sometimes dredged up from scattered memory – without thought, his mind somewhere else until the geography became fixed in place and hardened there. Each instant as significant as the corners where two roads meet, as rigid as a street address. He bought a road map and started to draw in each small dot, yellow for fires, sharp bright red for accidents, black for deaths, threading thin lines between them. But it became obvious the map wasn't big enough – the lines ran together, and instead of helping him keep track, they confused him.

So he made a bigger one, blowing up sections on the fire chief's photocopier. The new map was grainy and grey, but had far more space for each mark, each small handful of careful, crabbed notation. He kept it in his dining room, spread on the big maple table, the dark, empty tall-backed chairs standing motionless, silent observers. Soon, he had to stop eating there. He found the map overpowering, his eyes drawn to it, and away from his plate.

And sometimes, he found himself avoiding the room entirely, as if the map had taken on a life of its own in there. Instead, he'd sit in the dark in his truck near the fire station, the red coal of his cigarette the only light except for the dancing numbers on the department radio, numbers that skipped up and down the scale and stopped when nearby departments went out on calls.

His pickup sat on the shoulder, but Hennessey was moving down the road in his head, counting off landmarks along the way. Four doors up and five months back, a hose had burst on a propane barbecue, and the dancing flame wrote a cryptic, blackened script message across a cream-coloured garage door.

Jodean had packed that day, while he was out, taking her things and some of theirs, leaving the packing tape and knife on the counter next to each other, as if she had stepped out, halfway through something, and might be right back. He had wandered through the house later, trying to make sense of the language of what was left and the text of what had been taken, trying to read something out of absence.

Five houses further down the road, and a seventy-eight-year-old man had cut a tree down on himself, one bone-white branch stabbing into his back and pushing his shirt out in front slightly, just above the chest pocket, and the man tried to explain how it had all happened through a froth of pink bubbles that gathered and burst on his lips. Hennessey remembered that, for some reason, the man was wearing a white dress shirt, speckled with sticky, aromatic spruce chips from the chainsaw, and leather work gloves stained black with chain oil. Trees one, loggers zero, he had thought, and he knew they'd laugh at that back at the fire hall. And he could see the sky and the white wood chips flying, while he held a pressure dressing against the old man's chest to slow the bleeding and the other firefighters carved the tree apart.

His mind seemed to skip ahead, bouncing from place to place, faster and faster as the spaces between events narrowed. Where two lost boys had walked out of the woods; the path where a dog had fallen from a cliff, chasing the fast shadow of a jinking black mink. A chimney fire that had burned like hell's breath, showering him and another firefighter with clinkers and flaming chunks of soot, the heat of the fire eventually lighting the walls inside the house right through the brick confines of the chimney.

He found a pair of shoes later in his closet, one lone pair of strapped sandals in the back of a closet, pressed tight together, as if they had been placed there to be found.

Soon he could close his eyes and move along catastrophes connected by geography and disconnected from time, so close together that the map was almost unnecessary, each event like a rosary bead on a long and unforgiving thread. But still the calls came, and he charted out disaster's course, looking for some sort of order in the clustered dots that sprang up. Sometimes he would find himself staring down at an empty spot, wondering whether something was out there, waiting, like a flipped coin finally falling towards heads. It was, he thought, a complex calculation, a message in a foreign language. If he could somehow grasp the sense of it, find the order in it, he would know where to be, and maybe when.

He found a half a grocery note in a drawer, her handwriting, the list of what they needed abandoned after apples. He started driving to places where nothing had yet happened, sitting in the dark in the truck, breathing in the summer night air, listening keenly to every sound while the trees rattled. He found excuses for not eating anything that needed to be cooked, throwing apple cores and the stubby remains of pears out the truck window, and some nights the cab of his pickup smelled like a mix of cider and old cigarette smoke.

And one night he stood in his living room, looking out at the dark shadows of the trees across the road but seeing a Volkswagen lying on its side, the driver's door ripped off and a front-seat passenger lying on the yellow line in the middle of the road, mewling, his leg pointing south but turning dramatically and unnaturally east just below the knee. The driver in the ditch, face-down and quietly drowning in three shallow inches of water.

Then someone was talking to him, standing behind him, so close he felt the touch of her breath behind his ear, and for a moment, he thought he was listening to Jodean.

"Am I cut bad?"

But there was no one there, at least, not at first, and then, like being pushed into the wind, he was back again, back in the ditch. It was like the dreams where he would sit up gasping, images still sucking at him while he pulled – willed – himself awake, the sweaty sheets bunched around him.

He could spread his first two fingers apart on the map and span the space from the girl in the ditch to a spot where he became sure there would be a farming accident that involved hands and sleeves and a drive shaft, an accident so graphic he knew he would remember it mostly in the abstract, working on autopilot. Once there, he knew there would be bursts of colour and fear, and each step would be by rote from his training, without ever thinking of the difference between a hand and what he was holding. It was like that, the memory often more a collection of shapes and colours, of texture and warmth, sound and smell, than it was of any ordered reality.

"Cut bad?" he heard. "Am I cut bad?"

Then the night came when, all at once, he was fully dressed and standing at the end of his driveway with his hand on the door handle of his truck, already picturing a van on its side with someone thrown clear and then pinned underneath the vehicle, but his pager was silent and the night was warm on his skin. There were no sirens – there had been, he realized, no call at all – and the moon was edging up over the hill, backlighting heavy grey clouds and edging them yellow-white.

And he decided he was done with maps. Done.

The smell of heavy rain coming hung in the air, tasting like tin at the back of his throat, and there was a tang of crushed juniper close around him. The night was still and breathless, and there was no need anymore for any event to anchor his memory. He felt almost light then, and he sat near the edge of the road and watched the moon trace its gentle arc, felt the heat running out of the ground below him, and watched the rain coming west to east until the clouds overcame the moon.

The next morning, he cleared the dining room table, balling up the great grey map and stuffing it into the garbage in the kitchen. He tied the bag, and took it out to the edge of the road. He backed the truck down the gravel lane and drove to work. Then he was humming, the truck trembling slightly as it sped up on the narrow rural road. Small trees were in bloom on both sides of the road, and the air was fragrant with the must of dogberries, the fresh and sharp smell of the spruce trees warming.

And perhaps, he thought, it wouldn't really be so hard to go out, if the other guys asked again. Downtown for a beer, not that much to ask. Maybe it wasn't too late to go back to the easy good nature there had been in the fire hall, when they would make bitter and cruel jokes about the things they had seen, and then almost fall down, they would be laughing so hard.

A bumblebee, its legs wrapped in pollen, hit the windshield. And another. Two great, flat, yellow-white dots. And his chest felt tight, as if his body was suddenly being wrapped in tiny, tiny taut strands of string.

Still driving, without breathing, he reached out and, with the tip of his index finger, traced a thin line between the dots on the inside of the glass. Just like that, it all came back in a rush, the cold realization that there is no forgetting – ever – what you already know, that worlds undo and lives unravel. And it was Jodean and a ditch, and crashed cars and hands and people who could no longer summon the strength to even bleed.

"Am I cut bad?"

And for the first time, for the very first time, he realized how deep, how very deep, the cut had been.

Perchance to Dream

WHEN IT STARTED, I HOPED IT WOULD BE just a couple of nights, that it was something I wouldn't really have to worry about. Because what do you do when you're afraid to sleep with your wife? When you're terrified of what might happen there in the bed between you?

You know how it is: I had a dream where someone handed me an old two-dollar bill, the kind that's out of circulation now. Then, the next morning, buying coffee, the man in line in front of me handed the clerk just that kind of bill – I haven't seen one in years, and maybe you can say that's all coincidence. And really it is – the first few times. Then, it begins to seem like a message – and after that, you get afraid, wondering just what it is that's going on in your head.

I'm forty and happily married – we're among the lucky few, the kind of couple who, when we have people over for dinner, realize afterwards that one of the guests has moved things around in the medicine cabinet, searching for dirty secrets. But we don't have any. Twenty years in, happily married, and wondering why we're the ones who get to be happy. And worrying, too, worrying about whether it all will turn on a dime – whether we could find a way to mess it up. Until then you trust, and hope. We've got two kids old enough to have their own lives, old enough to ignore their parents, anyway. David, the youngest, is about to turn fourteen; his older sister, Rachel, sixteen, is caught up in a world where parents inhabit the fringes of the universe.

"Do you have to go now?" Anne asked while looking away, something she didn't realize was always a hint that she knew the answer already.

I'd been planning since two in the morning – a bunch of places I could go, but nothing pressing. Nothing except the dreams. I manage money for a bunch of clients, most of them pretty well off, so I set up meetings and I fly out to see them. Most of the time, the meetings are really formalities – they nod and try to listen, and then I keep them ahead of the taxman and any ex-spouses.

"Yes – no choice. Clients pay the piper, so they call the tune." The words sound hollow the moment I say them, trying to keep my voice jaunty.

Truth is, I'm on the road on a made-up errand, and I hope to keep going until the dreams stop. The first one was bad enough.

A dream about knives – just knives. The way their handles looked, black and rough and wound with something that looked like tape – I knew I was supposed to pick them up. Pick them up – and the dream was packed with such incredible dread that I knew something else was going to happen if I did.

I woke up staring at Anne's naked back, at the point of her shoulder, her skin dark against the backdrop of the cream-painted wall, thinking for some reason that pushing a knife through flesh couldn't really be that hard. And I was shaking.

The sensible thing would be to try and get some formal help, I suppose, but how do you explain to anyone that you keep dreaming about killing your own family? It's only dreams, after all, and that's what any reasonable professional is going to tell you. And what kind of help do you get? I don't know how anyone else would feel, but I think it's a little stupid to rush off to the doctor right away, when it's something that might just cure itself.

Still, maybe there's something in there – something in my head, I mean, like some sort of chemical imbalance or a tumour or something. That would be a simple explanation, but it's hard to believe because there's nothing else wrong. If a doctor were to ask, I'd have to say no problems with appetite or desire, no weakness or pain or anything. Normal bowel movements, for Christ's sake, as if that mattered at all. At first, I was afraid of just how stupid I'd feel, trying to explain this to someone else.

Then, the next night, when I did sleep, I was putting burned bodies into body bags in a burned-out basement – I remember, because I was having so much trouble with the zippers. And it was important that it be done fast, because the bodies had to be moved quickly. All three of them.

And those dreams, as unsettling as they were, marked only the beginning. Now, they seem almost trite and under-done, as if their author hadn't completely thought them through. Luckily, by the time the really terrifying ones started, I was already on the road – I'm sure I made the right decision about that.

First, to Nova Scotia, to a client who lives in his own small cove – he's bought most of the land around him and I have the feeling that I really only handle a small part of his portfolio, that there is a legion of other managers out there just like me, facelessly competing for our slices of the pie. His name is Art, and he dismissed me with a wave of a hand in a huge, wood-lined living room with massive windows looking out over the salt water.

"Go ahead," he said. "Whatever you think," as if he couldn't really understand why I'd made the trip in the first place. Smart man. It gave me a chance to turn the car towards the highway, a chance to drive myself to distraction.

I hope Anne doesn't start putting together where I am, and try to sort out which clients it is I'm supposed to be seeing. She might decide I was making it all up to see a lover, although how there could possibly be anyone I'd want more than her, I'll never understand. I think about her and my right hand goes straight to my left, turning the warm circle of my wedding ring around and around its finger. Three or four times every evening on the road, I think about the warm curve of her back, her calves, what she'd look like, standing naked in front of me in yet another hotel room shower, and then I deliberately force those thoughts out of my mind, because I'm afraid I'm setting the stage, drawing her out of the wings and making her part of the main event in yet another night of dreams.

I felt a little giddy when I reached the end of a long, sunlit Nova Scotia day. I'd driven three hours or so in a rental car, pulling over when my eyes got heavy. The drive would normally take an hour and a half. Every time I pulled over, the moment I went to sleep, I was awake again, terrified.

I stopped, waiting, in a parking lot, looking for the chimney swifts. I hope I'm waiting at the right chimney, a standing brick column in a Nova Scotia town, the building torn down but the unused chimney kept as a swift hotel. They're nothing special, just a bird I've never really seen up close before, with the benefit that they deliver themselves right to you.

Wolfville is where a former hockey player lives, a player whose finances I stickhandle while he runs a sports bar he's decorated with his own sports memorabilia. It's a good idea – if you want to see his Stanley Cup ring, you can, and you can have passable clam chowder and cold draft beer while you're doing it. And he serves his own bar most nights, and doesn't mind having his picture taken with patrons. It was not a project I would have recommended, but I certainly would have been wrong about that one. It made money from the start. Darren doesn't hold that against me, and I move the rest of the money he saved from eight years in the majors around and bring him a pretty solid return. Right now, it's a return he's happy to just reinvest.

At dusk the swifts return after flying all day without a rest, file straight into the chimney by the hundreds and disappear – there is an archetypal story about where the birds over-winter, how, in the 1940s, scientists banded them with metal bands, tiny metal rings. And then an anthropologist working in Peru found a tribe wearing necklaces of small metal circles – the bird-bands from scores of swifts. The swifts hang in their Wolfville chimney by their claws and by quills in their tailfeathers, and I can't help thinking how apt it is that one man's scientific curiosity is another man's dinner.

Sleep is a scientific curiosity, too, but I'd much rather have a meal of it.

I check in at a rather formal Annapolis Valley inn, a hotel made out of a rich man's house, so that many of the rooms have fireplaces, and many of the bath-rooms are an afterthought, the tubs claw-footed late additions with new copper piping coming up ragged through old bedroom floors. My bed is old and suits the room, and the mattress sags into the box spring so that you feel as if you are falling into a human-sized hole. It is rapturously uncomfortable, and I spend hours looking at the ceiling, at the pattern in the plas-ter, until finally I fall asleep for a few moments, just long enough to dream about tying complex, tight knots around someone's thin wrists – and their neck.

Then, the next day, I leave the car at the airport and fly to a big hotel in downtown Toronto. Holed up in one of a thousand faceless rooms, I feel like a worker-bee, trapped inside a hive. It's a concrete box with a king-sized bed, an iron in the closet, and an automatic coffee maker with enough coffee for precisely two pots – one decaffeinated, one not.

This time, my client doesn't even have time to see me on such short notice. He's doing a building deal, one of those complicated shuffles that involves zoning, city council, and buying land before its owners realize the potential might change – so I go out alone for Thai food, spicy chicken that leaves my mouth burning for hours. The client doesn't really understand why I'm there, or what there is to talk about. I could hear irritation in his voice, a tone that says, politely, what-exactly-are-you-doing-here?

That night, it's a simple dream, but absolutely terrifying. I'm cutting meat into small cubes, the way you would to make chili, but there's something wrong about the meat, something you can't really put your finger on, something familiar about it. And it's cold to the touch, and that makes everything infinitely worse.

I wake up and it's still dark, so I wrap myself in the bedspread and go out and sit on the cold concrete of the balcony to wait, shivering, for dawn. The sun comes up pale over the city, the horizon almost silty with smog, and I watch the light change through a palate of soft smudged colours, pinks and browns and bruise, until finally it's time for the taxi ride to the airport. I'm thinking about sleeping pills now, wondering whether or not they'd give me a clear, clean slate of sleep or whether they'd just trap me down there, half asleep and half awake, so that I'd feel like I was drowning in the dreams, unable to surface because of the drugs. That idea seems so frightening I'm not even willing to chance it, not willing to risk opening my mouth and not being able to make any sound come out.

Four hours on the plane and I can't wait to get off. Two teenaged girls next to me when we get on at around six, and they're both sound asleep within minutes of takeoff. They don't need headsets or movies, and they sleep the sleep of the dead, their mouths agape and their legs stretched out in front of them, unmoving. I get to watch them occasionally mutter and shift, and once in while they open their eyes briefly and then their lids flutter shut again. I hate the fact that it's so simple for them, and I want to shake them gently and tell them that they have no idea what a benefit the simple pleasure of sleep is.

In the mountains, I've given up on even the pretense of seeing clients. I've flown into Calgary because it was the first flight out of Toronto that I could make, slapping down a credit card and bolting from the city as fast as I could. After that, another rental car and a drive into the mountains.

I check into the first resort hotel I come across in Banff, it's got "Villas" in the name but I can't even remember the rest – and the room is strikingly familiar, except for the mountains outside my window.

The hope is that I can distract myself from the night-mares, that I can beat myself into exhaustion in the thin mountain air and then just topple over. It's a long shot, I'll admit. Maybe two hours' sleep in Toronto, so things are getting a bit scattered now.

In the bathroom, I have two beer in an ice bucket, and when the melting ice falls with a slightly musical clatter, it's like I have company without any of the bother of making conversation. They say you shouldn't drink when you're having trouble sleeping – I don't know if that applies to nightmares as well – but I'm tempted to simply pour the liquor into myself – drink until I gag, until I just fall over, to wake up later with a mouth full of too much spit and a head that feels as if it's packed with painful gauze.

Instead I go up into the mountains, the dust rising in clouds around my feet on a trail following the prints of other walkers, and, eventually, the small, sure prints of mule deer as well. The air is as dry as the dust here, and once I get high enough, I can see the coil of the Bow River heading down through the valley, and the mountains are all bright white where the sun hits the stone. I notice that everything feels like I am touching it through saran wrap, as if I'm not quite reaching it. There was a restaurant one of my clients took me to in Toronto once, a steakhouse where they brought out all the possible cuts of meat on a cart, each cut wrapped tightly in saran so that it couldn't leak and make a mess. It had a kind of surreal effect: meat without really being meat. I can't explain it, but I suddenly feel distanced from things, and I wonder if it is the lack of sleep. It's got to be – it can't just be the air, although I notice it feels like I am pulling the air into me every time I walk up even the slightest incline.

If I sit up late enough, perhaps my sleep will be black this time. But I now know that you can sleep in armchairs, and be just as tormented as if you are laid out flat.

And in the high, thin, dry Rocky Mountain air, I open both bottles of hotel hand moisturizer and rub it all over my arms, my back, my chest, trying to stop all of my skin from sloughing off in flakes. I feel like a burn patient, absolutely raw. Peeling. It's funny: the thought passes through my mind that my entire skin might come off the way a lizard sheds, leaving a perfect sleeve of me behind. For some reason, I find the idea hysterically funny, and I laugh until I can barely breathe.

That night, I dream of a perfumed shape behind a backlit curtain, a shape that's dancing, and that is eerily familiar. Nothing remotely frightening in that, except my job is to find the narrowing in the shape that is a neck and squeeze it hard.

I'm glad I am alone, because my body feels so slick that I would burst from a lover's arms like a watermelon seed from between her fingers. And besides, my hands feel dangerous.

I sleep again, I'm sure for only moments, and I dream of pulling saran wrap tight over someone's mouth, and I wake up thrashing.

It throws me out the door into the Rocky Mountain cold, and a thin mist has come down like a curtain with the night. I see shapes on the road that I can't be sure are there. Two deer, a mother and young, and I see the grain of the asphalt, the way it knits together into a whole, and I think that is important, but I don't know why.

Trying to go without sleep is a bad idea – ridiculous things seem sensible, and you come up with solutions you'd never consider otherwise. Rationally, I know it's a bad idea, but I don't think I have many options at this point.

After twenty-four hours, it's like spending a day fasting for medical tests – clear fluids only – and waking up the next morning and feeling fantastic, giddy, purged.

Over breakfast, someone tells me that the mountain valley is supposedly so filled with energy that native tribes would only pass through, refusing to stay. Now hail pelts down outside, and it's late May – I bet the natives were more concerned about the weather.

Big eagles fly up the valley here, and I try to talk sensibly on the phone about what I'm seeing. Bald eagles, not that rare, but they are set high against a backdrop of snow-toothed mountains, so that their clockwise lazy turns define the bowl of the valley. That message doesn't seem to communicate well.

"When are you coming back?" Anne says on the phone, almost pleading. She is talking slowly, as if she thinks I'm not getting what she's saying. Maybe I'm just talking too fast – I don't know.

I want to shout over the phone line "I'm keeping you safe!" but I can't find a way to make the words make sense.

After I hang up, I realize I'm shaking again.

The drug store has three kinds of wake-up pills, the sort that students take before exams to try and make up for all the studying they haven't done. I buy one of each, take double the recommended dose of the first box and wash it down with a black coffee.

Perhaps there is a reason I'm not meant for the company of others.

But I can only do this for so long. Sitting on the balcony watching the rain fall, I see a face in the falling drops, even though I am awake. My fingertips feel like they are fizzing, like I have my hands in club soda. The housekeeping staff keep rattling the door-knob – I think it's the housekeeping staff, but I'm not going to check – I've got the Do Not Disturb sign up, but they keep coming. I see the shadows of their legs through the crack under the door – I don't know what they'll do if they get in. They'll see my bed hasn't been slept in and they'll call someone. I pull the covers back, but it looks like an invitation. I make the bed again. Try to make it look untouched then. I have to keep coming back, straightening the edges, pulling the ripples in the comforter until it all lies flat.

Maybe Anne has called them – she must not understand.

I just won't do it. I won't sleep. I will hold on as long as I can, and I will beat these dreams. I'm flying south tomorrow, towards the us West Coast, still hoping.

A simple night, but longer than I expected. Easier to watch the television with the sound off, to watch those yabbering mouths clapping open and shut, because the noise clatters around in here as if the whole place were ceramic tiles. Phone off the hook – when the message light begins flashing too brightly, hurting my eyes, I put one of the pillows over it. Don't need pillows anyway. Waiting to drive to the airport early. Jumpy now – I go for a walk in the night again, and even the silence is oppressive.

The drive, no problem – I don't remember any of it, except for the billboard with the smiling woman. For some reason her stare almost puts me off the road, like she's trying to talk, like the bright lights of the sign are pulling the front of the car like a new kind of gravity. I can talk to myself, I don't need company – sometimes I talk too loud.

The things you learn: screaming on planes, they don't like it. I was only asleep for a moment – I let my guard down.

In the dream I was cutting with a knife and smiling – I saw myself smiling. Red rooms and a deep thrum like a heart beating, but not my heart.

I phone home when I can, but I have to hold my teeth tight together to sound like myself. Sheer willpower, to make the words come out as close to normal as possible. To me, it sounds like someone else talking.

"Don't worry, everything's fine. One meeting in Seattle, and a couple of days on the coast." Keep it light and simple – it would be easier if I had written down what I want to say, but it's hard to read my handwriting anyway – I've been keeping track of the wake-ups I've taken, but some of my notes look like little vibrant coloured snakes. And sometimes the hairs on my legs all shiver at once, like a fairy wind, like a bug is crawling up towards my knee. I slap at my legs absentmindedly, before I realize what I'm doing.

"Will you be back for David's birthday?" Anne sounds like she's been crying: her voice is thin and dry, and it wavers from word to word.

A sharp pain, that. Birthdays – remembering David's face at seven, watching the wonder of him open presents at two. The image is as strong as if he were toddling along right there in front, a vivid colour slide show of a tiny perfect boy. As clear as if it were happening right then – I'm sure my eyes are open, and I'm sure I'm still staring at the back of the phone booth. He toddles towards me, clutching a stuffed Big Bird, his hair the bright platinum curls it was until he turned three. So clear that I could almost talk to him. But he's thirteen now, fourteen in three or four days.

"Of course I will."

I think I left my luggage at the airport, either that or it was stolen from the trunk of the rental. I don't remember getting it back, but I'm not sure where they take it when you just leave the flight. I'm thrown off the plane in Calgary before they can even close the doors, and I can see from the anxious faces of other passengers that they're glad to see me go.

Getting another rental car is easy, because the computer's in the way and she can't really see my face. My face like steel now, because I can't stop grinding my teeth, like rolling a fistful of marbles together in your pocket so that they grind with a vibration that is almost a noise. Almost a colour, really, a sheet of white with curved vertical black lines. I can find cards in my wallet, the plastic necessities. Driver's licence, VISA card, "here are your keys," and out to the lot for a mid-size, burgundy this time, and I try putting the seat all the way back – just in case – put it up again and all the way back, looking at the dome light and the fabric of the inside of the roof, and when I sit up again, the lot attendant is staring at me, and I wonder what he's heard. When he picks up the phone, I wonder who he's calling, so I turn the key, put the car into drive, and whip out of the lot so fast that I almost nudge a pile of luggage two cars down. The radio searches for its own stations, so I turn it up as loud as I can. Power windows. I open them all. The air rolls in my ears like shallow thunder.

Getting out of Calgary is hard, the houses all look like teeth in a big head, all cream-coloured and virtually identical. The problem with coffee is that you piss almost as much as you drink, and I'm pissing on tangles of wildflowers, small blue nodding ones on long blue-green stalks, on small daisies and yellow flowers – bright little suns – that I've never seen before. Down below me is a driving range, and I can't tell if the green is unusually speckled with odd round flowers, or whether the golfers have buckets of yellow golf balls. That's funny, too, and I piss for hours.

Then I lose a day – a whole day, only it's night again and I'm still driving. I should have warning lights on the car, like those "Wide Load" banners, front and back. "Danger – Sleepless Driver," and somewhere I've crossed the border. It's funny: I can think of the border guard's hat, the pole-barricade, and that he asks a lot of questions – but I can't remember the questions, or what I say. There are other flashes – a firetruck screams past me, going the other way, and I see a firefighter in the jumpseat, facing backwards, driving towards danger, looking bored.

Sometimes it's the interstate, wide and straight and surrounded by heavy trucks, and sometimes smaller roads, trees right up to the shoulder and looming. Can't decide which I like better. On the big roads, the trucks passing make me twitch and lurch suddenly towards the shoulder. It's like finding someone right behind you, whispering in your ear, when you didn't know they were there. On the small roads – too close to the centre line, always, sometimes across it all at once because you can't help but feel you're being pulled into the ditch. Can't decide – drop the cups over the seat into the back, or pitch them out the window. Giggling uncontrollably at that. Bought a whole pie somewhere – half of it is on the passenger seat, no seatbelt. Not much of a conversationalist, though. It's depressed – it's blue. It's blueberry. Christ, that's funny. My fingers are stained blue – must not have bought a fork.

I'm doing well, though. Haven't slept yet. No dreams to speak of. Sometimes the shapes of stuff on the side of the road turn out to be something else once I get closer, but that's only sort of like dreaming.

Wind up at a highway motel in Washington State. I rent a room and abandon the rental car out among a forest of semi-trucks, some of them with engines grumbling, lights still on. It's a motel built around a big gas station, bright and all lit up like a spaceship landed here on the highway, and it's sucking people in like some kind of big ant-trap, baited with huge clean bathrooms and fresh coffee. There are shower stalls and even bunks and there are truckers everywhere, wolfing down bacon and eggs at three o'clock in the morning, snoring, shaving in the sinks. It's like they live on a different clock, but so do I. I have my own clock; it's just hard to read the numbers.

I have a room near the reefer trucks, the noise of their refrigeration units a drone like big sleepy bees, a noise that swallows up other noises and leaves the night empty.

The mini-fridge has four kinds of beer — I make coffee.

I must have left the door unlocked, and there's someone using my bathroom. I thought it was locked, but I'm drifting in and out. The person comes out of my bathroom, and sits across from me in chair, just like that, as comfortably and easily as if she belongs there.

It's a woman — a small, thin woman, but pretty in a fragile kind of way, dark hair cut close to her face. Addict-pretty: high thin cheekbones cut her face the way rocks sheer, abrupt and all along one clear fault line. She says her name is Lisa.

"They call us lot lizards," Lisa says, and I don't know what that means. It must show in my face.

"I turn tricks with truckers. For money, for drugs. For a room for the night."

And she sits down on the bed next to me. Her sequins shine red in the light that comes through the blinds – sequined tube-top over small, high breasts – and I think of hummingbirds, especially ruby throats. I tell her that I am dangerous, that I don't know what will happen.

And she laughs. Peals of laughter: laughing the way that gives you hiccups or makes you want to throw up.

"I know dangerous," she says finally, "and you're just not it."

We agree that she can sleep in the bathtub with all the spare pillows and the blanket from the closet. She's a tiny thing, shorter than the tub, and she says she's used to a lot worse that that.

"Just pull the shower curtain if you have to have a piss," she says.

"Yeah, I wouldn't want to embarrass you…"

She laughs again. "It wouldn't be me that was embarrassed," she says. "You haven't got anything I haven't seen."

Disarming how someone so small can take such quick control. She has sharp white teeth and a pro-nounced underbite – pretty, but she also looks some-how feral.

I tell her about the dreams and her eyes are wide for a moment, and then she nods, like she's hearing about a particularly familiar disease.

"I dream about slitting throats," she says. "About giving some trucker head and then cutting off his dick with a straight razor while he's still hard, saying to him, 'How's that, then?'

"But I haven't done it yet." She smiles. Pretty girl.

"Dreamt about lots worse than that," she says, shrugging. "But they go away. Just dreams." Sometimes her face looks much older – as if she's focusing on something just ahead of her eyes that I can't see. I've run out of wakeups – threw the last empty box out when I rented the room. And suddenly it's like my head is full of molasses. There are still thoughts in there, but each part of them has to pull out of the soft ground in my head, making a sucking sound like boots in wet soil. My vision goes flat, into two dimensions, so that Lisa's face is like a panel in a comic strip. My eyes are crossing.

We're sitting on the bed then, and she pushes me backwards towards the pillow with both hands, so hard that I feel the imprint of her hands long after she's taken them away.

There's someone I should really call, I think, my head filling with black. Someone I should call, so they know I'm all right, so they know where I am.

"You'll sleep," she says, her voice close to my ear and urgent, and my eyes close hopefully, almost a reflex, believing she's right. And I do slip away, faster after the pinprick inside my arm.

Just before drifting off, I try to tell her about Anne and the kids, about what I am trying to do, but my tongue feels so thick, pressed against my teeth and refusing to form any words at all. No one is really listening, because I'm not really talking, it's just that my brain is making shapes like words that don't go anywhere, they just run around the inside of my head, thudding into the surrounding skull and then sliding down into a pool somewhere near my neck. She's holding my left hand, sliding off my watch, my wedding ring. But my arms are like dead weights, and I can't imagine she can hold even one up for very long.

I wake up again later, and she is filling a syringe with liquid from a saucer on the table – "We'll share," she says – and then I sleep again.

Musical Chairs

HE LOST THE FIRST TWO FINGERS RIGHT AT the knuckle – the index and middle fingers on his right hand – in the chattering chain drive that carried half-made, tapping hardwood chairs around the plant.

Another one, he lost later.

He was holding the chain, putting a chair on its hook after attaching the legs to the seat, when his fingers caught.

And he probably would have kept both fingers if he hadn't lost his balance at the same time in the loose shavings, slipping the clutch and popping the chain back into gear. Lying on his side on the floor as the bright blood sprayed over the loose curls of maple and birch, he half-saw the fingers as they juddered away, bunched together in the greased chain. He lost sight of them forever when the chain rolled over the first spindle, although he saw that last chair travel all the way to the varnishing station.

A handful of brand-new chairs there, lined up as if ready for a children's game, but sticky with varnish so no one could sit on them.

The chair plant was almost a hundred years old, a long, leaning one-storey structure held up by rough-hewn timbers inside and covered with greyed shingles outside. It was bunkered between huge piles of sawdust and shavings that the company burned in the boiler in winter for heat, but the shavings piles always grew, supply outstripping demand, and occasionally the plant workers would be treated to hot, smoky fires in the yards that huffed like giant's breath and were started by spontaneous combustion deep within the heaps.

Then the loaders would turn the shavings and dust as if tending God's compost, and the company would pump hundreds of gallons of water up from the slowly-curling river to put the smouldering blazes out.

The same loaders brought the dry maple and birch logs to the front of the plant, where they were cut and planed and spun on lathes, getting ready for the chair assembly.

At the end of the chain line, near the loading dock, the company's name, Black Rock Furniture, was branded into the bottoms of the chairs, and the smoke rushed fast and dangerous from the hot iron and the charring wood. Fine sawdust covered all the equipment like flour, sifting down into the cracks on the floor and crusting up his nostrils, and the workers, mindful of the risk of more dangerous, explosive fires, had to have their smoke breaks outside where the gravel road widened to let the 18-wheelers turn around and back into the loading dock.

They smoked looking across the Gaspereaux River, a low, flat, rocky river whose flow was determined by the distant hydro dam that provided power for the chair plant.

In summer, the air hung low and still, and the cows moved slowly up and down the sloping pasture on both sides of the river. Higher up the hills were the hardwood stands, silver-sided and grey maple and paper birch, and the stands ran back across North Mountain, past the single-wide house trailers at the ends of the woods roads, past forgotten, hard-scrabble orchards doomed to fail, past the grey-sided woods camps bleached by the sun.

Finally it was just solid hardwood and the curious white-tailed deer, easily-startled grouse and hares, and paths that led nowhere.

When David Hennessey came back to work, the two blind knuckles made him something of a celebrity, even though, when he was among people he didn't know — like when the labour inspectors came to ask him about the accident — he would hold his hand in a fist out of sight behind his leg or pushed deep in his trouser pocket.

And that celebrity was an unexpected surprise.

Small incidents from the past had always made Hennessey feel like an outsider, like the way that, on the loading dock, the two guys who worked without shirts in the summer – Bill Roundtree and the always-spitting Lorne Boutellier – pushed by him roughly when he stood in the open doorway on his break looking at the water. Pushed by, and looked at him hard from the corners of their eyes, as if daring him to start something they would love to finish, just for the novelty. Boutellier had broken someone's nose for the first time when he was in grade nine: that was also the last year he had gone to school in nearby Gaspereaux.

Or at the Christmas social, where Hennessey sat alone and drank his way through the nine red cardboard free drink tickets the company handed out in a row, all beer except for one too-sweet glass of white wine for the Christmas toast. And the women from the line all turned down his requests for a dance – Elaine Boutellier, Lorne's sister, in tight, tight jeans and a western shirt, three snaps unsnapped down to right between her jutting breasts, said "Come on, Dave," dismissively when he asked, as if he were telling her an old, familiar and not-very-funny joke. Peg Godden and the DeVries sisters, all three of the women from the sanding station, had said no without even looking at him, watching other men on the dance floor and then laughing among themselves about something as Hennessey walked away.

The only thing he took away at the end of the evening was a door prize, once, a set of barbecue tools and a joke apron that read "Here's the Beef" and had a bright red arrow pointing straight down the front.

He put it in the second drawer, one down from the forks and knives, the drawer with the glue and unplanted carrot seeds, with the barrel-fuses for the oven and the replacement Christmas light bulbs he never took out of the package.

But when Hennessey came back to work after the accident, something had clearly changed.

"Did it hurt a lot?" That from Bette Godden, a gluer, one of the small, angry-looking women who spun like tops around the gluing station where the spindles went into the chair backs and were fastened tight. She had never even spoken to him before, but now she stood close enough that he thought he could feel the heat of her, like a quick and burning furnace, against one side of his face.

"Not much," he said, although it wasn't even close to being true.

His knuckles were purple and angry-looking then, and in some half-remembered, incomplete way, the pain still swam in front of his eyes like a red film when he thought about it.

For a while everyone talked about it, about how the crew had taken three quarters of an hour to find and fully disentangle the pulped fingers, and one of the workers had thrown up after seeing the mangled digits. About how, as the ambulance was leaving, everyone else had sat on a row of finished chairs in the loading dock, watching. Whenever they all sat outside, there were always too few chairs for the number of workers, leaving one or more standing.

They sat looking at the white, tissue-thin apple blossoms and waiting for health and safety to come and inspect the equipment, and someone turned the radio on, country music tinkling out of the small, tinny speaker, and the workers who weren't sitting fidgeted and walked around.

They lost a full day on the line, and some of the glue had hardened in the abandoned glue-gun nozzles, and a whole set of the nozzles had to be thrown away. They had tossed cigarette butts into the river waiting, and sent the office assistant into Black Rock for more smokes. And Lorne Boutellier from the loading dock had killed a young, brown-speckled gull with an artfully-thrown stone the size of his fist.

Later, Hennessey started smoking, too, holding his cigarette between his ring finger and his pinkie, and the scar tissue stood out hard and waxy-white where it pulled taut across the bony sockets.

Somehow, the scars became an introduction to the others, to the loose semi-circle of smokers who kicked around small talk about weather and sports, family and enemies.

Dave, who had always taken his breaks standing off to one side, found himself more and more often sitting in one of the finished chairs they drew up to the very edge of the dock. He liked listening to the stories, especially after the weekend, like the time Viv Morris had gotten wildly drunk on vodka-and-seven at a barbecue at the Goddens and had tried and failed to strip off her own pants, her fingers hopelessly confused by the button-fly of her new jeans. Or about a dust-up at the Anvil tavern in Wolfville, where Lorne Boutellier ran into yet another university kid who hadn't heard of his reputation, so became unwilling victim number nine in Boutellier's collection of mashed and broken noses. And one summer day, the sun high and everything wilting under its heavy hand, Dave even thought for a moment it might be nice to own his own barbecue, thought that he might have some people from work up to sit outside his North Mountain trailer, that they could sit and laugh and pitch empty beer bottles far back into the woods.

It lasted through summer, while the apples fattened and bowed the branches in the orchards, and Hennessey began to be able to flip names into his conversation – "Lorne" and "Kym" and "Viv" – and sometimes he forgot what it had been like before, and was almost able to relax.

The plant was running flat-out by then, boards being clamped and glued and shaped into seats, the legs and crossbraces and spindles turned on lathes and then set into drilled holes by the gluers, and the strange and damp mystery of the bowed backs made of long, thin strips of birch soaked wet and then bent on hot presses. The steamers sweated like longshoremen in the vicious wet heat, considered themselves craftsmen, and wouldn't sit with anyone else. Finished and half-finished chairs travelled along their chain-driven journeys, and their legs clattered together with hollow, singular notes, notes that all combined like a particularly forceful army of wooden wind chimes.

Then, just as summer was ending, a lathe operator named Morgan from further up the line dropped a smoke in his own lap on a tight, rural-road curve and rolled his red Chevrolet pickup into the tops of a row of midnight spruce trees near the South Mountain. And when the truck rolled, a case of twenty-four James Ready long-neck beer in the front seat flew through the air, all of the bottles breaking, turning the inside of the cab of the truck into a kaleidoscope of broken brown glass, foam and blood.

The truck hung upside down for an hour, swinging gently back and forth in the wind and dark, while the firefighters tried to figure out a way to get it down without doing more damage to its nearly-senseless driver, who mumbled swear words and bled slowly but ceaselessly from a zig-zagged collection of mostly minor cuts.

Morgan hung in his seat belt with a spectacular but inverted night view of the Gasperaux Valley and the North Mountain. And if he had cared to look, or had even known it existed, he might have seen the two yellow windows of Hennessey's trailer shining well up on the hill, back underneath the maples.

When he got back to work, Morgan's face was marred with rows of black nylon caterpillars where the doctor had picked out the brown glass slivers, the rows of stitches marching across his face like monotone cross-stitch. He lisped because he had bitten through his tongue, and the first thing Hennessey heard Bette Godden ask him was "Did it hurt a lot?"

"Not really," Morgan answered, the nylon caterpillars writhing with the words.

Hennessey flicked a cigarette butt out towards the river, but it fell short.

The next day, Friday, he was late coming out on lunch break, and, wouldn't you know, there were no empty chairs left on the loading dock. Unwrapping a ham sandwich, Lorne Boutellier swore at the music warbling out of the small radio, stretched as far as he could while still sitting and slapped the radio off its perch on a packing crate, silencing its thin song permanently.

Everyone was teasing Morgan, telling him jokes, trying to make him laugh, because every time he laughed, he'd wince and moan "ouch, ouch" as the unforgiving stitches bit into the edges of his raw cuts. Morgan was almost encircled by the group, and Hennessey could see that every single person was looking at the lathe operator.

The trees that might become chairs moaned around Hennessey's trailer on windy nights, and when they did, he could not sleep.

Three and a half weeks after Morgan crashed his truck, the wind woke Hennessey near two AM, the hour of bad decisions, as a fall storm danced lightning along the Gasperaux. He got out of bed, dressed in underwear and a T-shirt, the lights browning and brightening again as the lightning plucked absently along the power lines, and the rain outside sounded like gravel on the windows.

The drawers near the sink were made of thin plywood, painted glossy white, and the top drawer with the knives always stuck.

He stood next to the small kitchen table, his mangled hand flat, two fingers and a thumb spread on the red and white plastic tablecloth. The taut skin over his knuckles hurt, the bones in his hand throbbing with the weather-ache.

He held the narrow filleting knife for a long time, the long, thin blade winking in the irregular light. The table had one short leg, and it tapped the floor lightly when he pressed his full weight down on the tabletop.

Tap-tap.

It didn't hurt that much.

"Not really," he murmured, pressing a cloth against the newly-raw joint of his knuckle.

"Not really."

He put the knife in the sink, and looked out the window towards the trees in the dark, hearing the wind clack the saplings together. Imagining Bette Godden asking, then imagining himself looking down at the empty knuckle, shrugging unconcernedly and telling her brusquely, "Accident with a knife."

And after he parked his truck on the first day back to work, he pulled his hand carefully and gingerly out of his jacket pocket, holding it out so everyone could see. He could hear the chairs already dancing on their chains before he even got in the door.

Heartwood

FIRST, IT WAS CABINETS.

He had talked her out of buying them, said he didn't mind the time it would take if she could wait, and it was her first year at the new school – "I'll be busy, John, so you'll have to do most of it on your own," Bev said.

He was, he thought, ready for that.

"Not much work around now anyway," John said. "I can work away until things pick up."

First birch, with its clean, green smell, that almost-wet sharpness, even when the wood was dry. John Hennessey had stacked it with spacers in the shed for three months, reading the moisture with an electronic gauge that barely touched the wood with its two tines before offering up its verdict. He wanted quarter-inch birch-faced plywood for the doors, and he didn't want the framing to warp or pull away.

So he waited, and ran his hands along the smooth face of the top few pieces of wood, already feeling the beveled edge he would cut with the router. And sometimes he would hold the solid and dependable wood up to the side of his face, smooth against his skin, its grain running true except for the occasional small, dark eye where a branch had anchored to the tree. There was something about the running flecks of the grain, gapped occasionally so you could fill in the spaces with the fine edge of a fingernail – for John, it was as if you could see the wood packed tight with energy, waiting to burst apart, held together only by the tensions of its internal structure.

It became almost like a conversation while he waited – every few days, checking, touching, and sometimes he would talk, too, self-consciously at first, urging the wood to dry, checking the stacks, moving spacers at the first sign of anything close to warping. Inattention, he thought, would not spoil this.

He built the boxes of the cabinet backs first, and hung them in the kitchen on a night when Bev was out, so there was no one to help him lift the awkward rectangles into place on the wall, no one to hold the level or watch the wandering little bubble inside the light green glass tube. No one to watch the crucial plumb line he had chalked along the wall to mark where the edge of the first cabinet should go, that one straight line upon which everything else depends. It was a warm September evening, and he had the windows open, the first strong winds of the fall swirling the dust on the kitchen floor. It was curriculum night, and Bev was meeting with the parents of her grade three students, everyone crammed into the tight little chairs in her classroom.

"You should see them in there," Bev said before she left. "Get them in the door, and the conditioning kicks in. You can see they have to fight putting their hands up before they even ask a question." She told him about the discipline problems, and about a boy named Mike who vomited whenever he got picked on. She talked about the new teachers that year, and how more and more were women. "Male teachers are almost a rarity now," she said. But she didn't ask about the cabinets.

So John held the cabinets as best he could against the wall, one-handed, the tendons poking out along his arm in long lines, and with his other hand he used the stud-finder to try and find the two-by-fours inside the wall.

He thought of the stud-finder as wood-yard alchemy: no batteries or lights or power cords, just a small magnetic tumbler that wavered straight when the device was pulled across a stud hidden behind the gyprock. A magic wand to tell him the right place to set the screws so that the cupboards would stay solid and fast and true.

Even after the doors were varnished on the outside, he could open any one and notice the smell of trees amongst the canned goods and dishes, as green and fresh as if the sap might just at that moment have started to run.

Once the cabinets were in place, he thought they hung as if they had always been there, the styles cut and curved to match the molding in the kitchen, each run of the router as even and long and straight as the doors themselves.

"They're nice," Bev said when the cabinets were finally finished. John had to admit he'd hoped for more than that, but he'd brought her into the kitchen right after she got home from work.

"You're tired," he said, looking across at her while they ate dinner. "Want me to run you a bath?"

"That would be nice," Bev said, smiling ruefully and putting down her fork. "But I've got marking and lesson plans for tomorrow. Not enough hours in the day." That evening, she worked at the kitchen table – he drew up new plans, paper unrolled on the living room floor, hardly a word between them.

The cabinets were the first – the first project he did alone. The work was both satisfying, and unnervingly different. They had painted rooms together, newly married and still able to laugh about paint spattering on their faces when they were doing the ceilings.

They had fought bitterly with wallpaper, joking that it was the next best thing to divorce when the paper soaked too long and stretched, leaving the edges never quite an exact match. And they had made love on the floor, urgent and wild among the paint cans and plastic drop clothes, then bathed in the tub where the black-and-white ceramic tiles hadn't been grouted yet, laughing and trying to keep the water from splashing.

In the empty rooms, even before furniture, he could remember looking at her profile against the glass, her tongue stuck slightly out between her lips as she concentrated on painting the window trim, and he had felt an ache he couldn't describe, a piercing ache that felt for an instant as if it might be the last thing he would ever feel.

But they both were busier now, so they worked together less and lived more like two planets inhabiting the same wobbly, misaligned orbit – and sometimes he worked late and fast and careless, the cuts on his hands deep and slow to heal. While his hands paid the price, the work was as flawless as he could make it – each line measured two or three times, his tools sharp and clean, all details planned carefully ahead of every cut or nail.

After the cupboards, the pine floor – wide boards that he edge-nailed through the groove, watching the straight lines multiply as he moved slowly across the room from the windows. Fresh, dry pine, white now in its first unbarked exposure to the light, and the room had the close and rich smell of resin. Already, he could picture how the boards would deepen and yellow in the sunlight, how the colour would grow rich with age.

And Bev went off to a Saturday teacher's inservice, smiling and waving a loose, limber-fingered wave as she walked easily down the long gravel driveway to the car. She held the car keys ringed around her index finger, the silver bright in the morning light.

"It just doesn't get easier," she said. 'You understand, don't you? It'll be better when I'm used to the school, when they're used to me. When I'm on staff instead of on contract, and when things are going better for you."

"You mean when I get a job?"

"No, just when there's more work, that's all."

He watched her go, the morning foggy with warming mist rising up off the road, and then he threaded another long strip of nails into the power-nailer, started it up and listened to the familiar bull-dog chuff of the compressor.

Alone with his cross-hatched stacks of pine boards, he took the wood one piece at a time and used the miter saw to cut out the worst of the knots, the fat, ringed black knots that spoke about how old and huge the pine trees had been. They had grown fast, the grain wide and healthy, whispering now about hot summers past and plenty of rain, about long, sharp, deep-green needles and stretches of New Brunswick forest where the ends of branches meet for miles.

Looking at the ends of the boards, watching the rings curve and cup, sighting his way down the length of each one, he could imagine the sawmill, the planers, the spinning sharp blades.

One by one, the boards marched in a flat regiment across the floor; soon they reached almost from wall to wall. Bev was still not home – but there were complex angled cuts to be made around the base of the stairs, and he lost himself suddenly, falling into making pencil notes on scraps of brown kraft paper, trying to find the intersection between the abstracts of geography and the fixed orbit of grain and length.

He had the windows closed, worrying about the humidity, worrying that the boards would gap apart if the room dried too fast, and he was in his sock feet, humming and dancing at the ends of the handles of the huge rented floor sander, when Bev came in. There was no way to hear each other over the roar of the sander, and it had to keep moving, back and forth, to keep the sandpaper from chewing into the soft, pitchy wood, so he waved to her, and she waved back, stepping over the sander's cord. With everything overlaid by the noise of the sander, it was as if she floated up the stairs soundlessly, every motion precise but out of reach. He wanted to go upstairs too, and talk to her in the bathtub – just to sit on the closed toilet and see the soft brown of her shoulders against the tiles – but he stayed downstairs instead and sanded until he was sure the tub would have filled and the water had been turned off.

Sometimes, they managed to say "good night" before he fell asleep, exhausted, or she turned away.

Cherry, then, difficult to find in such large pieces, hard to the touch and brutally unforgiving, but he had a long, over-heavy board that could be cut and pieced together like two side-to-side halves. Even when it was dry, the sawdust had a smell that was foreign and bitter, a tang that spoke to him of wet, fresh green trees, like a memory of that first feral smell of spring. Bev was going to be out of town for the entire weekend, so it was a good time to cut the board and glue it together, letting the glue dry before planing the great wide board flat. It was a wood that had to be caressed, had to be worked gently, and he saw in the wide, assembled board the seat of a chair, waiting to come out. He laid his chisels out all in a row, yellow handles pointing towards him, the frighteningly sharp blades that swept through the wood pointed away and resting on soft flannel.

His eye followed the grain easily, his hands knowing instinctively when to press down, when to let the chisels flow along their found arcs, and when to stop. The weekend fled, swept up in shavings and dusted with sawdust from fine-grained sandpaper. When Bev came back, he showed her the beginnings of the chair, while she leaned against the counter next to the sink and slowly drank a tall glass of cold water, her body a long, straight line angled from the floor to the front of the cupboards.

He told her about finding the curve of the seat, and she nodded, bottled up in her own thoughts, he guessed. He told her about the sweep of the chisels along and through the wood, but the tools were already rolled up in their flannel and put away in the toolbox, and he had a feeling that she didn't really understand what it was he was talking about, as if he had suddenly learned a foreign language and couldn't help speaking in it. He thought that she was nodding politely, but finding no sense in his words.

"So what's next?" she asked, but he thought she was humouring him, and he was sure she didn't listen to his answer because she looked away towards the window as soon as he started speaking.

In November, he found four great long pieces of maple, the grain tight and whorled like the thin brown skin on the outside of a horse chestnut on that first day when you peel it out of the spiky green casing, fresh from the autumn tree. Boards you only find once, honey-brown and complex inside, telling a long and complicated story about the nature of the sun, about scraps of nutrients drawn up through small and questing roots, about the cold stasis of winter and the eager rush of the thaw. Run smooth through the planer, he thought he could hear voices there in the wood, that if he pressed his ear tight against the grain, he would hear a single ringing tale from shoot to stump. Sanded fine and polished, the wood had a curious depth, so that looking at it was also looking into it, the colour and flecks of grain creating their own small and balanced universe.

Bev was away for two more weekends, an in-service for math and another for the new religion textbook, and in the quiet of the house, he decided to use the wood in a tabletop, knitting the boards together into a flat and heavy panel that he cut into a long oval. The wood was so hard that it took a finish like glass, the polish making the wood seem even deeper. The tabletop was like a pool of golden water in the sun: looking down into it, all sorts of life seemed caught in mid-movement, a sheet of fractured and lined amber. Every time he looked at it, it seemed different, more involved – and he found it completely impossible to explain. Especially to her – Bev would watch him sometimes, offhandedly, and he thought she was watching the way you might look at a construction project you drove past every few days, as if the building were springing up almost magically by itself.

It wasn't until the table was finished, the maple flat and singing in the dining room sun, that she told him.

There had been no weekend meetings, there had been almost no meetings at all.

"I've met someone – Kevin Squires. He teaches grade four – we've been seeing each other since September." She looked at the floor, and then back up again. "I'm leaving at the end of the week."

The words came out in a particular order – set in place: later, he would remember that – as if they had been practiced over and over, as if they had already been said repeatedly to the cupboards, to the furniture, to the floor. Thoughts hurled through his head faster than he could say them: "You couldn't do any better than someone else in the staff room?" he wanted to shout, but then he looked at his rough hands, the criss-crossed tool marks and broken nails, and his eyes centered on a splinter driven in deep under his right thumbnail. It was surrounded by a plum halo of blood, somehow making him realize that he was standing there still grained with workshop sawdust, scarred with the futility of it all. And he spread his arms out like branches, as if to say that he was all around her, built into the walls and the floors.

"You keep what you like, okay? Keep whatever you like," she said. "You decide."

"I want to keep you," he said stupidly, already feeling how heavy and wooden the words were.

"Well, that's not happening. You've got … whatever it is you've got here, and we'll just go our separate ways," she said. "A clean break."

John couldn't say anything. Stuck in one spot, he watched her head for the stairs, watched her turn towards him, her heels hard against the floor, angry.

"You're dumb when you're in love, okay?" she shouted at him as he stood there. "Just dumb."

And John realized that he should have known already. He realized that he should have known for weeks, that he should have seen the pattern, watched it rise practically in front of his eyes. That he had watched the fugitive grain, without ever knowing what he was looking at.

Wood-yard alchemy.

Later that night, there was a high silver moon, and he stood up late by the bedroom window. The trees stood still and growing and quiet, lighted silver-grey all along the sides towards the moon, pencilled as black as coal along the sides away. The curtains hung still and straight, and the moon traversed a gentle, lazy curve through the night, while the branches stood reaching, their grasp turning with every inch of the moon's glide. All of that made sense to him, order, line and even shadow, while nothing about her now made any sense at all. He knew that it had made sense before, it had been so simple that he could feel her in his hands without even touching her, without a thought.

And then, even later, as she lay sleeping, when he was sure she was sleeping, he ran a finger slowly across her back in the dark, looking for a plumb line, the one straight line upon which everything else depends.

I want...

THOSE ARE THE BLINDS I WANT, THE WHITE-painted wooden-slat ones, the ones that always hang so straight and even and close out the brightest sunlight, leaving straight, thread-thin lines of light on your skin when you lie still on the bed. And I want that note of wood smoke; the fine, high tone of birch logs burning that you smell outside on a cool fall day, the air sharp against your cheeks.

Driving endlessly by at night, I can see through the window that your house has a cup-rail high along the living room walls with small-framed pictures on it, and that the room is painted a dark red – maybe burgundy, maybe even deeper. It might be too dark, really, but in summer it must make the space feel cooler, as if it were permanently in the shade. And I can see the plants, piling over themselves, lush and rich and obviously well cared for, hanging down over the edges of the pots in loose green dangle. There's too much to them, a richness that overflows. The pictures are too small to make out, and I drive by far too fast, but I can imagine they are like small Scottish landscapes, dark and dour and pursed-lipped, punctuation more than illustration.

At night the windows are all in reverse, transmitting instead of receiving. If only your house was the one for sale, that's what I think. I don't know you, really, but there are things that are clear, that I know from just looking.

I've seen your husband – I guess he's your husband – and I've seen you and your little boy. I've seen you laughing, and I've seen the way your face falls into an easy, calm, familiar pattern when there's no one else around, when you're out digging in the flower garden along the foundation.

Sometimes I want to stop and yell, "Don't you think anyone else has ever thrown a damned ball?" but I realize it would be wasted on you, that I'd just seem like a disturbed old man in a silver truck. That you'd be frightened and call the police, when all I really want to do is to warn you. Sometimes I just want you to know that other people know the happiness you're feeling, too, and that sometimes it rattles around inside them and keens like the winter wind. I want to stop and warn you that it won't get any easier, that the angles will always grow sharper, the disappointments more distinct.

I've looked at other houses, lots of them, and I know all the real estate signs. Red and blue, white and green. I know the faces of all of the agents in the newspaper guide, too, know which ones will answer their cellphones on the weekends and which ones will wait until Monday, even if it means losing a sale.

I imagine they all know me – I imagine they get together sometimes and roll their eyes. "Had a viewing with Ivan Hennessey," would be all one would have to say, and the others would nod and understand.

Because I'm a serial viewer, a St. John's openhouse haunt, the constant wraith that never actually gets around to writing out an offer.

And it's not because I never see what I want, because really, I'm easy to please. Nor is it that I can't afford to buy, because I can – if you've got a good job and you're walking around with $60,000 worth of divorce settlement in your pocket, there isn't much that you can't look at around here. There's not much that's truly off the table.

But you can be paralyzed. Sometimes you crash into stuff. An accident in a marriage is as easy as being rear-ended at a stop sign. One moment, you're going in one direction, measured, slowly, 'til death do you part. The next, you realize everything has changed, and that the expected suddenly isn't. That your back won't straighten right any more, that the pain won't let you sleep for any more than four hours without waking you and kicking you right out of the warm sleeve of bed. And two o'clock in the morning is just as desolate when you know exactly why it is you're still awake, when you're waiting for the pills to dissolve. When you realize that you know the geography of a new and small apartment so well that you can fly around it in the pitch dark never even touching a wall, like a pilot flying on instruments only.

You don't get to put the pieces back together the same way, because they don't fit anymore. One moment, you're outside watching your boy toddle around the yard, chasing the flinging, desperate grasshoppers, and the next, you're living alone in an apartment with a foreign kitchen, where the spoons are never in the right drawer, where you look into the cupboards at a mystery that you seem unable to make sense of.

I've put the palm of my hand on the rough lumber of basement stairs in a hundred houses just to remember what it felt like. You can feel it now, if you think hard, that rough, resisting prickle. And that's not all. I've caressed newel posts, let my hand slide down bannisters, and I know the fast slick of varnish, the resisting grip of shellac. Shellac was originally made of bugs, you know. Maybe you don't know that – that it was a resin excreted by the lac insect, until chemists found their own way to make it.

And maybe you don't know that the best of it is not the empty houses, that it isn't the ones you have to furnish with truckloads of imagination.

The best ones are the occupied ones, the ones with the full shelves of liquor, the ones where you wonder just what kind of occasion really calls for Sambuca. The more pieces to the puzzle, the better –

I love the houses with the fugitive cats that gaze down balefully from the heights of closets, or that dart away quickly in ginger streaks, anticipating a kick. The houses where someone's underwear is dangling out of the clothes basket, or where the kitchen sink has enough dishes to let you calculate how many came for supper the night before.

I'm sure the agents think that I'm just never satisfied, that I'm looking for some sort of house that just doesn't exist – because I've looked at everything. From three-storey Victorians with the whole top floor wide open and a soaker tub, to squat single-level old-style homes with peaked roofs and hip windows. Just about everything, really, and I remember most of them, except for the suburbans, which all fall and fade into one. Built-in appliances, washers and dryers that always come with the sale, anything to try and hook the fickle buyer.

And it's not that I didn't want them either.

I've wanted every single house, everything in them down to the margarine tubs of screws and nails in the basement. Down to the laundry baskets in the hall that bulge with clothing tossed there without even a thought about the casual house-comfort it represents. The security of not wondering, the ability to just have without ever knowing what it is that could be lost. The plodding, wonderful drudgery of the everyday. The casual ease of workshops where projects are sitting only half-finished, where things are left to dry or to harden, where the only thing missing is a hand to pick them back up. Cardboard moving boxes, folded flat and tucked into corners, so that it is only occasionally that you get to read the Magic-Marker-ed directions saying "Kitchen" or "Front bedroom."

I've looked under stairs and behind closet doors, seen dry-cleaning hanging in its bags and nightdresses abandoned on hooks as if they were simply shed one day and never thought of again. Pillows, often still with dents. Rows of shoes and sneakers, waiting vainly for feet.

A legion of shower curtains, frayed bathroom mats and magazines half-read, left hanging along the edge of a bathroom countertop.

Sometimes, the realtors are busy – I remember one already on the cellphone, talking to the next appointment, and I lingered in the bathroom, look-ing at the toothpaste tube all messy around the cap, the toothbrushes standing in loose formation in a glass on the sink. Burying my face in a light-blue hand towel, hanging right there on the rack, and wondering if I was smelling detergent or someone's shaving cream. Some realtors like to leave you pretty much alone – others tail you, endlessly explaining the obvious.

"It's a small kitchen, but with new cabinets..."

"Not the biggest of rooms, but with new paint, it'd be brighter."

They're the mind-readers, the ones who are trying to divine your intentions from your expression, from the way you hold your body when you go into each room.

I don't get many of them any more.

Others are happy enough to let you stroll while they hover just within questioning range. I get them a lot.

Happy enough to let you wander, happy enough to let you wonder. Happy enough when you leave, and when you do, they all have business cards with their photographs in the left corner, as if their faces will somehow make them harder to forget. Except that the cards wind up being exactly the same – they pile up in a green glass bowl in the kitchen of my apartment, and I put the bananas on top of them.

Other things you remember better. There was a house with sloppy swastikas on the basement walls, poorly executed in red spray paint, and another where desperation had caused the owner to cut down through the concrete floor to lay seepage pipe.

"Ever get water problems down here?" I asked, waiting to see how far someone would go for a sale. "No," was the answer, "no problems with that," even though in one concrete corner, a sledgehammer and an axe were welded to the floor with furry rust, the kind of rust that only occurs when something has been fully immersed.

Another house where the owners were cleaning up, but where every step just showed off half-measures. The carpet cleaner plugged into an exten-sion cord, making it clear that there was a bedroom with no electrical outlets at all. A basement, emptied of old bottles and the leftovers of things that inevitably end up downstairs, serving only to show the whole back wall wasn't concrete at all, but just damp brown earth. Light blue carpet in the living room, pried up in one corner, just enough to show you that there wasn't a salvageable floor underneath.

"But look at that garden," they said, nudging me towards the kitchen. "You just don't get a garden like that downtown."

Tiled kitchens, painted kitchens, kitchens with cabinets from floor to the ceiling – I like the ones where you can look straight out a window from the kitchen sink, so that you can imagine doing dishes while you look across the quiet simplicity of the yard. Touring houses in the daylight, you never imagine that it might be night time when you finally get to wash dishes, and that all you might see is the accusing reflection of your own face against the inky black glass.

And maybe then someone drives by and looks at the other side of that glass, and imagines the way your hands must feel, warm and wet, deep in the dishwater.

The way it is when I drive by your house.

I've looked in your windows, watched the blue of the television reflecting from your ceiling – I've seen every inch of your life, bisected by the slats of your venetian blinds. I know the day when you bring the groceries home, the time in the evening when the light goes off in the back bedroom. But you can't even begin to know the frustration of it.

Sometimes I think I'm only half looking for a house, that I'm searching vainly instead for the simple irrational, quick-boiling irritation of someone else's puddle left on the bathroom linoleum. Your puddle.

I'm looking for the slow, even, annual metronome of leaves waiting to be raked, for the responsibilities that drag at your soul like weights, until that emptying moment when they are gone and you realize how much you actually miss them.

And I drive by and look, and think to myself that I'll be ready if your husband ever, ever puts the house up for sale.

It's the house – the house that I want.

When he goes, he can leave the furniture behind; he can leave absolutely everything behind.

In fact, I wish he would.

Big Shoes

THE HOSPITAL CALLED, AND THAT WAS THE first thing I knew about it. Sure, I probably should have known something sooner than that, but it's been busy so I haven't gone over as much as I could have.

The nurse who called said he'd appeared in the emergency room in a wheelchair, with socks on his feet but no shoes, that he appeared to have had a stroke, that he couldn't have come in by himself.

And I went down right away, I did, and you have to wonder what the government's doing with our taxes, because the place was filthy and crowded with people. My father was tucked into a corner of the emergency room like he was a piece of the furniture, covered with a ratty grey hospital blanket, his feet sticking out from under the edge, brown socks, one big toe poking through, tipped with a long, yellowed toenail.

I couldn't help but think that he would have been ashamed to have been seen like that – he used to put a tie on for a doctor's appointment, for God's sake, and wear his favourite brogues, expensive and brown and carefully tended – but the man in the wheelchair wasn't really like my father at all. All the good had been cut out of him: his face was collapsed in on itself as if his teeth and tongue had been stolen.

"Hello, Dad," I said, kneeling down in front of him and reaching for his hand. His eyes stared off into space, unfocused. He was drooling. When I felt his arm it was barely more than bones wrapped in skin. He grunted, but he didn't speak. One of the people sitting next to him moved so I could sit down.

The place was dismal, really it was. Mauve plastic chairs, two tables with tattered magazines and empty paper coffee cups. A television on a bracket up near the ceiling, blaring professional wrestling. A woman on the pay phone, talking loudly to someone: "I was smoking too much and I just didn't feel right, okay? So I called an ambulance, okay?"

A beefy man with his arm wrapped in an elastic bandage kept shifting his weight, and turned to the person next to him. "Three fucking hours and nothing. The doctors here suck anyway. If they were any good, they'd be somewhere else, makin' more fuckin' money."

My father's cheeks moved in and out every time he took a breath.

The nurse said his wallet had been pinned to his jacket under the blanket, his health card sticking up on end. There wasn't any money in it. Looking through it, I saw he'd cut my university graduation picture down to fit in that narrow plastic photo sleeve. Me in a mortarboard and academic gown, smiling uncomfortably, my last few seconds of higher education frozen in time. I always thought that moment was both his greatest pride, and, eventually, his biggest disappointment. I hadn't continued on to be a scientist or an engineer, just became another one of the endless fleet of mid-level managers. In human resources, the dreaded HR, what my father would certainly have deridingly called "personnel." He had never said a thing, but I always felt that it hung between us like a faint smell of something gone bad, that if he could ever bring himself to just tell the truth, he'd tell me how I had wasted my potential.

"My best guess is his stroke was about three, four days ago," the doctor said. "We're going to admit him for now, but he'll be going into full-time care. I really don't think you'll see much improvement." He shrugged. "But I might be wrong."

A nurse leaving at the end of her shift gave me more information about how Dad had gotten there: "A little guy brought him in," she said. "He walked funny, like his shoes were too big."

My father had been a scientist, world-famous in the way scientists are now: renowned in his own little corner of the scientific world, something to do with the way nutrients pass through plant membranes. Important enough that the condominium was full of scientific papers and framed, dusty honorary degrees. Well-known enough in his own branch of science that, when someone on the fringes of plant biology heard my last name, they'd ask if I was related to him. I think he would have preferred it if the tables had eventually turned, and people had started asking him if he was related to me.

They gave me my father's keys at the hospital, so getting into the condominium wasn't a problem: I had my own set, of course, but you can't always put your hands on keys right away – they were probably in my kitchen, but I couldn't remember the last time I'd actually seen them.

His door, when I got there, was latched, but the deadbolt wasn't locked. I'd seen about getting that deadbolt installed after he'd made such a fuss about a few break-ins in other condos. Just kids, probably, after jewellery and CD players and camera gear – the kind of thieves that sweep through and move on – but you couldn't tell him that, because once he makes his mind up, the discussion is finished. The world was going to the dogs, that's the way he looked at it, and you just had to be prepared.

So it was strange that the bolt wasn't turned. Stranger still, once I had the door open. The place was a mess – well, more than the usual mess, anyway. His eyes hadn't been any good for years now, so there was already a permanent kind of disorder to his place.

You'd eat a candy from the dish at his place at your own peril: they could as easily have been put out a year ago as last week. Things would be on the floor that he'd dropped and hadn't seen. Before we'd agreed that candles might not be such a good idea, I'd occasionally come in and gather up small handfuls – like pick-up-sticks – of lost strike-anywhere matches.

But this time, the mess was different. Somehow, it looked more involved, more thorough.

Like any house, there were drawers that might not be opened for a full year: the box with the silver, for example, and the cupboard holding what had been my mother's tea set. But everything seemed to have been opened and then carelessly closed again.

The small kitchen was filthy, the garbage overflowing, dirty dishes piled in the sink. Every piece of cutlery seemed to be dirty; some of it was crusted and even mouldy. I was beginning to get really angry: it wasn't supposed to be like this.

The worst was the spare room.

The television I'd gotten for him a couple of Christmases ago was set up in the spare room, sitting on top of a slim silver DVD player I'd never seen before. There were dirty plates on the floor, and a plastic DVD box – porno – next to the light. The bed was unmade, the covers thrown back. The dresser drawers weren't quite closed, as if they'd been emptied and no one had cared to push them fully shut. Someone had been living there, that was obvious – but it looked like they weren't living there any more.

I'd been paying for home care, an arm and a leg really, and I tried call to the agency from the phone in the apartment. The phone wasn't working, so I made the call on my cell. They told me their file had been closed four weeks earlier – that Frank Otanski had called and said there wasn't any need anymore, that a family friend had taken over.

Well, I'm Frank Otanski, I said, and I hadn't called anyone.

"The last bill was paid off on Mr. Otanski's VISA card," I was told primly, including the $100 penalty for dropping the service before month-end.

I sat on Dad's couch for a few moments, dazed, looking at the dusty pictures of my brother and me. Stephen, who had done science in university, who even now was banding scared and puking seabirds on some desolate strip of sand off the Nova Scotia coast.

Just like Stephen to leave it all here in my hands. Sure, Dad thought the world of Stephen, but that did-n't mean Stephen actually did anything. I managed Dad's affairs, paid the condo fees and the home care fees, paid to have Dad taken to the doctor and the dentist. I did the work, and Stephen would fly in for a few days every four or five months like the lost sheep, and you'd think Dad's face was going to split, he was so happy. After a couple of days, Stephen would be gone again, and it would still all be on my shoulders.

Looking around the room, I suddenly realized what was different about it. It looked looted.

There was a space on the wall where there had been one small picture – a watercolour my father had bought my mother in an uncharacteristically roman-tic moment, a watercolour that had actually wound up being worth a few thousand dollars.

My father had pulled on his beard and smiled when it had turned out to be valuable. Proof to him,

I guess, that the rigours of science could be used to winkle out the answers to art as well. But it was gone, and so was the silver. Yes, family silver. Sounds trite these days, but it had been a full set of sterling silver, with stylized "Os" on the end of each piece – all of it in a rosewood box, set down in deep green velvet trenches. Murder to keep clean, probably black with disuse, but silver.

Every room was the same: just the valuable stuff was gone. Watch and cufflinks in the bedroom, chequebook and stamp collection. Candlesticks and coins and the healthy wad of cash that he kept under the head of his mattress, and could never be talked into putting in the bank. And something else – the shoes. The brogues, I mean. They were gone too – I should have noticed right away. They were always in the same place, just inside the door on a rubber tray. The tray looked bare without them. You had to know those shoes – Dad had spent good money on them, once, and they were one of his favourite lessons. Friday nights, he'd polish them with a brush and then buff them with a soft cloth, and the leather would come up as bright as glass. He'd had them resoled many times, and the tops were as soft and wrinkled as the skin at the corners of his eyes.

"Size twelves. You can tell quality," he would say, holding up one shoe. I'd never gotten much past size nines myself – my father was over six feet tall, and I was a good six inches shorter.

"Get quality, and it will last." Yeah, he'd say that, and with the next breath, it would be that the world was going to hell in a handbasket and nobody knew how to make anything good anymore.

But they were gone – and who the heck would take an old man's shoes?

One thing was for sure – everything else of value was gone. And whoever had taken it had plenty of time to sort out what was worth taking, and what wasn't.

Looking around, it was obvious that whoever it was had to have been seen by someone else in the building. But talking to the neighbours didn't turn out to be much help.

There was Mrs. Hennessey, who wouldn't take the chain off the door when she talked to me. I could see her nose and one of her eyes through the gap between the door and frame, and a slice – just one side – of her mouth.

"He liked Terry," Mrs. Hennessey said. Terry, who had arrived "a month or so ago," and had started helping Dad by moving some things from the condo down to the basement storage room. Terry, who had moved into the condo, Terry who had his own key.

Terry, who I had never even heard of.

No, Mrs. Hennessey said. She didn't know Terry's last name.

Down in the storage room, all of Dad's suitcases were gone. They hadn't been moved in years – I could see those brown suitcases so clearly in memory that I could imagine that there were marks on the dusty floor where they had been standing. I didn't know where the cases could be – but I was sure that Terry did.

Waiting for the superintendent to come down to his office, I thought about seeing my father in the hospital. It was hard to think of Dad like that, huddled and small there under the blankets. Not that he had been a big man physically, but he'd been big in a room, a presence, and he had been big enough, too, to push back out of the comfortable cocoon of professional science when my mother had died unexpectedly, big enough to be both parents to my brother and me.

I'd known the superintendent ever since Dad had moved in. His name was Ken, and I think I would have remembered that even if I hadn't been able to read it on his shirt. Ken brought a set of faucets with him into the office, struggling to pry the disk with the letter "c" off the top of the cold water tap. Ken was a large, square, helpful man, with hands so big it was hard to imagine them packed in under a sink, emptying the coffee grounds out of some old lady's sink trap.

"Terry moved out Wednesday," Ken said. "Nice guy. Handy with tools."

After Mrs. Hennessey's reaction, I didn't want to be too direct.

"So, did he leave a new address?" I said. "Any place I can find him? I'd kind of like to get in touch."

Sometimes people's hands freeze when something you say makes them suddenly think – it's like a curious, obvious silent alarm. I watched Ken's hands stop, the faucets forgotten.

"He was devoted to your dad," Ken said, in a tone that sounded accusing. "Helped him with the shopping, ran errands. Would even bring the mail up. Said that with your dad in the hospital, he'd be finishing up."

"You knew my dad was in the hospital?"

"Yeah. Terry was taking care of that. Said he'd make sure you knew."

Well, Terry didn't know my father had always hated hospitals, or that he hated them even more after my mother was admitted. I can remember watching my father swear in frustration while the eggs burned black in the frying pan in front of him as he tried to figure out the controls on the stove, and I can remember being late to school that day and many more. Men in his generation didn't ever have to cook, they moved straight from mother's embrace into the comfortable routine of marriage without even a pause – from coddled to cared-for without a step in between. But that didn't mean he couldn't learn.

Sure, he was lost at first: one day, Mom was there, and she could make home-made soup even though she was fading away so fast it was like she was making it out of herself. Standing there by the stove, wreathed in steam, her legs shaking. That's how I remember it – one day, she was cutting a whole chicken apart for dinner, breaking the joints backwards – and the next her own joints looked like the chicken's, knuckled out and bony, covered loosely with chicken skin. And then, just like that, she was gone. Not quite what a tenured professor usually expects, especially not my father.

"Said he'd come back to pick up any mail," Ken said.

"What?" I said, distracted.

"Terry. He said he'd come back now and then to see if there was any mail."

Would he, now? I'd be willing to wait and see. I looked on the key ring, and the mailbox key was still there, shiny and long – security keys, not the kind you can just get cut anywhere. Terry wouldn't be able to get the mail himself. He'd have to come to the superintendent – or to me.

Ken was watching me, his mouth turned down a bit at the corners.

"Mail comes around ten," Ken said. "Terry liked to be there when the mailman came. That's your best bet." When Ken turned back to the faucets, when his hands started to move again, I couldn't help but feel I had been dismissed.

After my mother died, my father could have hired help, could have had people in to look after us. Instead, he started to break a lot of rules, doing things that no one expected. Took Stephen with him to conferences in the States, took me at least once to Ottawa, where he talked to a Parliamentary committee about protecting seed varieties, while I chased pigeons in front of the House of Commons. We didn't think anything of it at the time. We weren't paying enough attention to realize that the other professors didn't bring their children to the departmental beer socials, or that we were invariably the only kids at get-togethers where the highlights were potluck suppers and the tweed jackets and the tie-dyed shirts all getting sopping drunk together on cheap Yugoslavian red wine.

He must have paid a price for that. Academe at that time had its own rules, and I know there were plenty of late nights where Stephen and I were the only kids toppling forward asleep into our dessert plates. Five, maybe ten years later, it would have been a lot different. By then, perhaps, it might have seemed almost normal. Ten years later, the rules were out the window, and plant scientists were doing crossover work with Mexican philosophers, and anything seemed possible and reasonable. Hard to imagine with the way things are now, but Dad must have been quite determined.

Every day, I tried to be at the apartment as close to ten as I could – and sure enough, three or four days later, there were a couple of letters addressed to Terry Traves, with my father's address on the envelope. Three on the first day alone, and I opened them all with hardly a pang – they were answers to a personal ad, all women. One with a picture: a dark-haired woman, pretty, looking half-on towards the camera with what was apparently meant to be an eager look. I threw it out – what I wanted was the picture he would have sent back to her. "Hi, I'm Terry. I'm single, white, and I like cold beer and making my living stealing from helpless senior citizens."

Bastard.

But that first day, there was no Terry Traves. The second day, there was a mailout from his parole officer, changing the date of his next appointment. Three or four days in, right on ten, a little guy came in, brown leather jacket and slicked-back hair, and I was out through the door and grabbing his sleeve, my other hand a fist, before he could even take the mailbox keys out of his pocket – but it was the wrong guy.

I hadn't even seen the pest control van until he started pointing at it.

Then, a few days later, a cheque came in the mail from a second-hand consignment furniture store – a big cheque. I realized then that I hadn't even noticed the long table in the living room had disappeared.

I could remember that table from before my mother had died. It was supposed to be left to me in the end, a teak table with ivory inlay around the edge. You couldn't even buy anything like that now, couldn't even bring it into the country because of the ivory. That's when I called the police.

The police didn't impress me any more than the emergency room had.

An hour and a half in yet another plastic chair, waiting for a Sergeant Parsons to tell me he knew just who Terry Traves was, but that he wasn't sure just what kind of crime – if any – had been committed.

"See, if your father gave him the stuff – or told him he could take it – then there's not a lot we can do," Parsons said. "He's an old man, sure, but it's not like you've got power of attorney or anything. He can do pretty much anything he likes."

Parsons was a big man, in rumpled white shirt. He was sweating. I knew why – like the hospital, it seemed like the heat just wouldn't stop. The whole place was a dump, overcrowded with too many old metal desks and wire baskets full of dog-eared paper and file folders.

"We'll interview your Dad, get his take on it."

"Well, that'll be a bit difficult," I said curtly. I know I was past rude by then, but I was completely frustrated. "He's had a stroke. He's not talking at all."

"Can he write? Is he expected to get any better?" Sergeant Parsons asked me.

"I don't know. I suppose he might."

"Then we wait. Check his bank accounts and change the locks, and we'll go from there."

Sitting in the hospital next to my father, I tried to count backwards through the days, to see how it could be possible that I hadn't seen him for more than a month. He was flat on his back, still not talking, an IV in his arm, the whole arm tied down to keep him from thrashing the needle out. I tried to imagine how it was that I could have been absent for enough time for this Terry to turn up and settle in.

At first, the math didn't add up. I thought I must have seen him about three weeks before, because on the first Wednesday of every month I bring over Chinese food. Then, before we start eating, he always tells me that it's not real Chinese food at all, that he had been at conferences in Beijing – he still calls it Peking – where you'd go and look at a bright red, plucked smoked duck hanging in the restaurant window, and a few minutes later, it would be out of the window and onto your plate.

But then I remembered that I'd had to cancel the last Chinese meal, that I'd been at work late and hadn't wanted to punch in another two hours of not measuring up with Dad. After that, I tried to piece together when it would have been that I'd seen him last, but finding the exact day was like those little floaters you get in your eyes sometimes – try to look straight at one, and it just flitters away. Your only chance to catch it is somewhere in your peripheral vision, looking at it while at the same time pretending to ignore it completely.

To be honest, maybe it had been a month and a half. Maybe, on the absolute outside, two months since I had last been over – but I had called more recently than that, I was sure.

Day by day, I was still collecting Terry's mail. No one had shown up to get it. No Terry, no one calling on his behalf – or, at least, no one that anyone in the building had thought to tell me about. Letters, the occasional bill, once or twice a cheque for something else he'd stolen. Once, a bank statement: little by little, I felt like I was getting a sense of the man, just by the pieces of paper that were trailing after him.

Back at the hospital, they'd look at Dad and say "at least he's breathing on his own." They used to tell me that three or four times a day, as if breathing carried its own kind of Olympic medal. There were others on his floor, on Four-North, on respirators, but Dad wasn't – and I was beginning to wonder just how bad he actually was. Every now and then I'd look at him and think I'd caught him pretending, staring back at me as sharp as a weasel. And then the moment would be gone.

It was hard not to reach out and pinch him. Hard not to say "Wake up. You're wasting my time here. There are things I'm supposed to be doing."

Once, sitting on that plastic chair, I'd even tried talking to him. At least he wasn't interrupting.

"I do my best, Dad. There's a lot that has to get done, and there's just me – I can't be here at your beck and call all the time."

Nothing – just breathing.

Before, he'd always been at me because I didn't visit enough. Always at me, and I never had the answers he was looking for: there's no way to explain where you have to be, when the only place you have to be is work. It's like you're speaking some kind of foreign language, as if your consonants and vowels have gotten themselves all mixed up, and you're spouting some kind of weird, incomprehensible job-based glossalalia.

But things were getting by me at the office – the work still had to be done, e-mails sent, evaluations done, and I was sitting next to someone who used to be my father, and showed no signs that he was anything of the kind any more.

Days passed, and still he couldn't talk. But even if he could, I got the idea that my father wouldn't be telling me anything about Traves.

Loyalties shift quickly – and old people are so damned stubborn.

Then one morning, as I got to the hospital with yet another handful of Terry Traves' mail, I met Sergeant Parsons leaving my father's room. He had a coil notebook in his hands, and he was flipping the cover shut, shaking his head.

"Still nothing?" I asked, trying to keep the opened mail out of Parsons' sight.

"No," he said. "No charges. Your father says Terry was working for him, that he gave him anything that's gone from the apartment as pay."

"Bullshit," I said. It just came out – I don't talk like that, but it was out of my mouth all by itself. The world felt suddenly tilted.

"Sorry," said Parsons. "That's what your father says."

"But he can't talk."

"Yes, he can," Parsons said. "To the doctors, since yesterday. To me, just now."

And the still-rumpled Sergeant Parsons stuffed his notebook into his jacket pocket and walked away down the hall, following the red stripe in the linoleum that led to the exit. I thought of that line as being coloured guilty red. Every night as I rushed away.

I pushed into my father's room, and I'll admit I was probably more angry than I had a right to be. I certainly said more than I should have.

"Who the hell is Terry Traves?" I yelled at him, throwing the handful of mail onto the bed. "He's not your son. He's not anything. He's just some con-artist who preys on the feeble-minded. Feeble-minded like you, Dad. I had the home care in to keep you safe from people like him.

"I put the locks on, and it did no damned good. You just let him right in."

My father didn't speak. I still hadn't seen even a sign that he could talk, that he could even move. They had him trussed right in with the sheets, pulled up high on his shoulders. He looked at me for a moment, and it seemed like his eyes were as black as night glass.

"You bought locks. You did the best you could?" he whispered, the words ragged and unsteady, as if his mouth was full of dust. "You bought the locks, and paid someone to come and put them on. Like everything else." And then his eyes swivelled away from me, up to the line where the ceiling met the wall, as if there was something more important there than anything else in the world. But there were also tears on his cheeks.

"I would have done it for you," he said quietly.

He wouldn't speak to me again, even though I sat there for the next three hours, until I thought from his breathing he must be asleep.

He looked impossibly frail then, even more fragile than he had in the emergency room, because suddenly, it was obvious he was still in there. Hiding behind that sunken face was the same person he'd always been.

When I got up from the chair next to his bed, I realized that Terry Traves' mail was strewn all over the bed.

And Stephen was finally coming, probably still smelling of birds, and I would have to hire someone to clean up the condo and get rid of all the crap that Traves had left behind. I'd have to get the locksmith in. Stephen would sit with Dad and jolly him along, and I'd be left racing all over the city looking for new home care – either that or a home where they could really keep an eye on Dad, whether he liked it or not. It would just go on and on. Then Stephen would up and leave again, and I'd be the helpless dope who even wound up booking his airport taxi.

And after that, I knew I'd still be out there all by myself, looking everywhere for a small man wearing really big shoes.

No Apologies for Weather

S HE HAD TURNED THE PAPER TOWEL ROLL around again, so that the sheet of paper came off the front of the roll, instead of the back. He knew immediately what that meant.

It was the same with the toilet paper in the bathroom – sometimes, for weeks even, it didn't matter which way it unrolled, and then suddenly it did. Leo looked around the bathroom: the towels were hanging with their edges turned under, and the toothbrushes were lined up in straight lines like a bride and groom waiting at the altar.

Not the toothbrushes, he thought.

There was wind outside, but the storm was still far away and building, an old man muttering about ancient, unforgotten slights. Gusty, slapping wind, but the early morning light was all sunshine.

Leo pulled back the curtains and let the light stream into their bedroom. Then he checked the closet. She must have been quiet at first, he decided. The sound of the hangers hadn't woken him, but all the shirts were now together at one end of the closet, pants at the other. The shirts were facing the same direction, too, their buttons all done up and facing west. On the floor, the shoes were standing at attention in mute parade, toes lined up square.

It was worse than he had thought.

The trick, Leo knew, was not to respond with bewilderment, not to curl up or hide, because that wouldn't do anything. Ignoring it was only postponing the inevitable. The trick was to do it right this time. To just do it right: to learn from past mistakes, to catch her while she was still falling, before she hit the ground hard.

Atlantic storms roll in fast, the first warning a thin petticoat of high, light cloud that spreads across the sky, unstoppable. One moment, there is that thin sunlight – that white, bright hard sunlight through a scrim of high cloud – and the next, the long green robes of the spruce trees have gone dark with frightened anticipation. Storms jump at you quickly, ripping the tops off the waves and throwing them in your face as salty spume.

The rain slashes down cold, almost horizontal, drenching you in an instant: the trees, large and small, sweep around together, branches moving as one, showing the wind direction like fast brushstrokes on loose canvas. Storms can be unexpected and dangerous, blasting you with snow and hail where moments before you had been revelling in the simple visceral pleasures of spring, and you have to take cover the best way you can. Sometimes the storms end quickly: other times, they seem to stall somehow, hung up on the shore and feeding on themselves.

She was somewhere downstairs, probably violently cleaning by now. He knew he would hear her if she was still upstairs.

It was a big house, two fat square storeys of dark green with white trim, large enough that two people could live at the tops of their voices and not disturb each other. Leo and Helen had bought the place for reasons that some of their friends found completely incomprehensible: the small coal fireplaces, the formal way the plaster was patterned around the ceiling fixtures, the banister that curved to the left, going up.

It was one of a line of St. John's rowhouses huddled on a narrow street. They had moved in six months before, throwing themselves into making the place their own, patching up the wreckage of their former lives as they patched plaster and poured paint into roller trays to cover up past mistakes. Past mistakes – they both had their own personal debris trails, memories blown apart and thrown willy-nilly on the ground by cyclones that had hit before they knew each other.

He knew she loved him wildly – knew it, without a moment of doubt. Lying in the bathtub, the hot water cooling around him, he would hear her singing in another room, and know that she was singing just about the idea of him.

She had picked up the pieces of his broken life, and had put them back together when he thought the very idea was a lost cause, swept the bits up and gently fit them back into a workable whole. She had taken such fine, delicate care that he had barely felt the touch of her fingertips – she had held him loose in her arms, knowing that she couldn't hold tight, and had told him he would one day be all right. And she'd been right. To him, she had a breathless magic that came with the rest, a bright brilliant light that was also accompanied by dark.

There was no way to tell when she had gone downstairs that morning. He already knew exactly what it would be like: guaranteed, she would be talking loudly – talking to no one.

Helen talked to herself almost constantly when she was alone, but Leo knew by now that there was a tone to listen for.

Down the stairs, walking alongside the high, white walls, trailing a fingernail along the plaster for balance: he was heading for the sound. That's what he always did, although, even before he got there, he felt a small flutter of fear in his chest, so familiar that it was almost expected. Still, he kept walking.

Then, he knew.

She was smashing dishes in the kitchen – at least, that's how he thought of it. Taking mugs out of the dish rack, banging them hard enough on the counter that he didn't see how, occasionally, a weak one didn't just surrender and fly apart into shards. Her back to him, she started stacking plates – smacking them together – while he watched. Making them pay for someone else's sins, he thought. He had never lived with anyone for whom so many things exploded – drinking glasses sometimes seemed to surrender and shatter, unable to contain the internal stresses of their form. Dishes broke, pictures fell. He had the feeling that anything breakable was just waiting, poised.

It was five o'clock in the morning, and she was already fully dressed for work – showered, her hair done, makeup on, dressed for an office that was still hours away. Outside, through the long kitchen windows, it was the kind of morning light that makes it seem as if the dawn is trying to make up its mind about breaking. The cloud thickening now, dense and solid, losing the delicate patterning it had when the cloud had been thinner. The big maples in the back yard were still black in shadow, leaning in like neighbours listening at the windows. Leaves starting to dance side to side in the freshening wind.

She was talking in one long angry sentence, and he knew it could be addressed to anyone: "If I told you something like that, you'd look at me and tell me I was an idiot so it's fair enough that I should call you an idiot, especially since I'm already doing all your work and you're always taking the credit anyway…"

Her voice had a low, angry undertone, a flatness, a sound that carried its own implied warning.

"Sometimes," Helen had told him once, "someone will pass me on the street on a bike while I'm walking and I'll realize I'm talking out loud, because they'll look back at me like I'm a crazy woman."

Helen had conversations with herself at full volume, sentences with full inflection and pointed edges.

He could imagine the bicyclist tottering away slowly, looking back over his shoulder, perhaps alarmed, while Helen was throwing out a late and apologetic smile. Even Leo could be shocked out of reverie: more than once, reading a book in the living room, he had been brought to his feet by an exclamation – "Don't think I don't know what you're thinking!" – from the kitchen.

Listen to the tone, Leo told himself as he reached the doorway to the kitchen. Listen to the tone. The subject doesn't matter right now, because the subject will turn like the wind bending through the points of the compass. Inside a big storm, the wind can cycle and come at you from any direction: the sound in the trees is your only honest warning, the thrash and whip of the leaves, the low moan from the eave-strough. It was dangerous to try and work from the words she was saying – take your cue from the tone.

She heard him then, sensed he was there and whirled around to face him, her shoulders square, her hands on her hips, by sheer reflex ready for an attack. Her arms were so very long that her elbows made perfect triangles pointing out away from her sides. Her feet were far apart, her balance solid.

She was an awesome sight when she stood like that: Leo always thought it was like looking at one of the nine Valkyries – and that, like the Valkyries, she had appeared to warn him of a battle he would not survive. But he wasn't afraid of how she looked.

Whenever he thought of her arms, Leo would remember holding her in the dark of their bedroom –

the smooth skin of the back of her forearm, the languorous way she would straighten and lay her arms back against the pillow after they had made love. God, she was beautiful. But he pushed that thought away as soon as it began to form in his mind – you can get into trouble that way, he reminded himself. Fast. This is no time for distraction. You have to be sharp, he thought.

"When you said that you were thinking seriously about the Ottawa job, what did you mean?"

Jesus. A sidewinder. He couldn't even remember saying that – at least, not that way. But she was always quicker than he was, especially on the ground that he thought of as offhand memory, and he knew he had to be careful now. He had to finger his way, feeling for handholds. But it was like playing cards in the dark – you can't even see your own cards. Her words were newly minted and precise, and they came out with each consonant clipped and neat. He knew that every word was carefully and deliberately chosen so that it could not be misunderstood or weaseled around.

There were no trick questions – no traps here. This was no minefield. All of the explosives were lying there on the ground right out in front of you, big and bright and nasty, Leo thought. The difficult part was seeing them and then not blundering right onto them anyway.

This was where they didn't mesh, he thought, the place where they always collided. The most dangerous of places.

He took too long thinking, he always took too long thinking, trying to find a complete answer. He started scrambling, knowing the silence just made things worse.

If he had time, Leo knew what he would have said: inside his head, the thoughts whirled with the wind, that he had thought about the Ottawa job — they had come to him, offered a bigger salary but a move that was hundreds of miles away — the way you think about all kinds of things when just getting an offer can be an aphrodisiac. It's not that you've chosen to do it, just that it's an active consideration that makes you feel better, that you can try on like new clothes. It's exquisite to roll around in the scent of being wanted. But that wasn't getting any closer to answering the question.

"Did you think about my job for even a minute in there? For a second? Did you think about me at all?"

He noticed the way her voice rose with the end of the sentence, "at all" rising to a peak — it was just the kind of observation that was so risky. Don't get distracted, he told himself. Don't get distracted. Give her the decency of the fastest, clearest answer you can put together.

"You don't spend very much time thinking about me, do you? I'm just some kind of Leo ride-along. Is that what you think?"

"No." He knew enough to say that quickly, that the bare question needed a bare answer. But then he stalled, as if someone had yanked on a hidden gearshift and dumped his mind into neutral.

"That's not what I mean about the job," Leo started lamely.

"But it is what you said. You said it last Thursday, and again Sunday in the car," Helen said. "We buy a house here finally, and you're ready to rip it all up and head for Ottawa."

"I don't remember saying it like that," he said, speaking carefully. It's a fantasy, he wanted to say, unsure of how to get that concept out. Five occasional minutes of empty dreaming. A fantasy where everything's new, and all your problems just disappear. But he didn't have a chance to speak the words. Outside it was raining – scattered rain.

"Do you think so little of me that you can just throw stuff like that out, without ever thinking about how it would affect me? About how it would affect us?" she said. Leo saw the argument hooking, saw the delicate bend, knew the curve it was taking would only mean trouble for him.

And promptly ran out of words.

Helen didn't.

"You're not really thinking about us in this, are you? What would you call it? Leo's Ottawa escape? I stay here, good wifey, while you go to Ottawa and find someone new to fuck?" Spoiling for a fight, now.

That's the problem when you know someone as well as lovers know each other – you know the soft bits, the spots where the damage can really be done. You know where teeth will leave a mark with the least effort.

And suddenly, it wasn't about answering her questions anymore – it was about running for cover.

Duck and weave, he thought, like a boxer. Guard your head and take the other punches wherever they land. He was taking cover on familiar ground, in a place he had been before. He had known it could happen this way from the moment he had woken up and found the bed empty.

In a real storm, a serious, violent northeaster, there is no shelter from the wind and rain. The trees whip flat and branches slap, and the wind and rain finds your face again every time you think you finally have it at your back. It curls and twists and buffets, and shingles start to flap, and then fly. On the ocean, streaks of angry white foam become solid ripping waves – waves without quarter, coming from all around. You're going to get marked up: the only thing you can really do is to leave as little of yourself exposed as you can.

And all at once, Helen was coming at him.

She halved the distance between them, and then halved it again. Shoved him with both hands.

"Or are you fucking someone else already? Is that it?"

There was no point saying anything now: she wouldn't hear it anyway. He knew she would only hear what was going on inside her own head.

That was it: how quickly everything changed, the way a switch flicked from light to dark. She was tall and strong and determined, but most of all, single-minded, caught fast and helpless in seething anger.

Brace yourself, he thought. He didn't know he had done it, but his hands came up and his back straightened. Her hands were low, and he couldn't guess how close she was going to come this time, whether she would stop inches away, pointing her finger in his face for punctuation, or whether she would keep coming, slapping or hitting. He turned his hip, protecting his crotch.

He wanted to hold her, to wrap her in his arms and tell her it would be all right, but he knew from experience that would be like holding bundles of reinforcing bar – that he was stronger, but that she would resist, focusing on the physical struggle until she had forced herself out of his embrace. And that would only make things worse.

His hands were out in front of him now, palms turned up, fingers splayed. He reached for her arm – she knocked his hand away.

With horses, you can see the whites of their eyes when there's thunder or when the wind rips whistling around their stables, heads switching back and forth, and their noses pointing high, nostrils flared. When they are right on the edge, just before they start kicking their stalls apart in an uncontrollable panic.

She had beautiful eyes, beautiful and hazel and set high over full cheekbones, but just then, he could see the whites all around her irises. And he was afraid that she'd gone too far this time, that she wasn't coming back, or that, worse, there would be no stopping her. He knew that he would not be able to hit back. And now, suddenly, he was afraid.

He would have been embarrassed to explain what happened next, even to her. How calculating he was: how deliberately he moved to the edge of the counter, so he could keep one hip against the cabinets to keep the cutlery drawer tightly shut. How, this first time, he kept his left arm only a short arc away from the kitchen knives, blocking her reach. How he kept that left hand out even as she started punching his chest – short, sharp-knuckled rabbit punches that would leave rows of small blue bruises – because it was truly the lesser of two evils.

Sometimes, storms end all at once. At their height, they suddenly pass, as if they wind up inside themselves and tuck their fury away out of sight, lightning darting inside the clouds.

His hands were tangled in her hair, her body was tight in against him and she was crying now. Her rage shattered like a fever breaks. It wouldn't be the way he would have described it to her, but it seemed to Leo that he could feel Helen deflating, could feel the fight draining from her.

Sometimes friends who knew, especially those who had seen her in full fury, would ask him why he put up with it. It would have been an easy question, one that took no time or thought to answer. He'd shrug, because it wasn't anyone's business. But the answer would roll around inside him like the echoes of thunder anyway.

"Because she burns like the sun," he would have said. Because every single thing, about her, good or bad, ripped through him like wonder and shook him by the neck. Because it was like living with the volume control up full and the roof down for every drive.

Leo held on every day for dear life. He waited for – and dreaded – every storm, and it engulfed him and amazed him every single time.

Sometimes, you can watch a storm pass, inch by noisy inch. You can watch its trailing edge scud away to the horizon, watch the blue appear, watch the confused whitecaps flatten as the wind fades.

The rain moves away and the wind slackens, an old man mollified now, only complaining for show. Behind the trailing edge of his coat, you can see sun, and it looks brighter than the sun has ever been before. The trees glisten with glasswater beads, and the air is full of the smell of bruised spruce and salt.

Leo knew quite simply that she was magic, and that magic can be both wonderful and terrifying. He knew it scared her as much as it scared him, that she was unable to explain it or stop it once started, and that she would eventually be left limp and exhausted, her muscles held taut for so long that they sometimes pulled and tore. And she would be sorry. Most of all, she would be sorry.

And she said it then, again and again, her words muffled so that he couldn't hear them clearly, but he felt her lips moving against his neck, and immediately understood that gentle Braille.

Nothing to be sorry about, he thought, stroking the back of her head while she cried. He knew without looking that every bottle inside the fridge would be turned label-outwards, that the lint filter in the dryer would be spotless, that every dead leaf on every houseplant would have been nipped cleanly away and thrown in the trash. That the trash bag would be tightly tied and put outside the back door, a new one in its place. He knew, too, that later, maybe tonight or even tomorrow, there might be thin, long parallel cuts on her forearms under her long sleeves.

If you live by the sea, you expect the weather, or else you move away.

"Nothing to be sorry about," Leo whispered. No apologies for weather.

Borrowed Time

IT WAS TWO A.M. WHEN THE VOICES STARTED. Low at first, so that he couldn't make out the words through the wall. But Frank knew what they meant – knew the angry tone and the way the words seemed to chase after one another.

She was listening again.

He had to resist the urge to get up out of bed, to bang on her locked door, to yell "I know what you're doing in there" through the wood. He knew it wouldn't help, knew that then the voices would lower to a mutter, maybe even less, but that they'd still be talking.

And he knew she was sometimes confused in the night, and that she had a shotgun in there somewhere with her – loaded with number six birdshot – and she might decide that he was dangerous and simply fire right through the hollow-core bedroom door.

It had been simple when he'd taken the job: live-in help for a little old lady whose hands were so bad she couldn't twist open new jars, and whose senses had faded so much she couldn't tell if the milk had spoiled until it was too late.

It was supposed to be simple. He didn't even have to be there all the time, just make sure there were groceries and that she got fed. The wages weren't great, but the living expenses were all taken care of: for a first job, just out of college with an English degree, he thought it was pretty good. And he hadn't given the big radio in her room a second thought.

"A nice boy like you not married?" Mrs. Pearson said to Frank when her son Paul – the lawyer – had introduced him as the new employee. And Frank had smiled and answered no, not yet, he was only twenty-three.

Mrs. Pearson snorted.

"When I was twenty-three, I was married and pregnant for the second time. You're just not putting your mind to it," she said. And then, "Hope you're better than the last one. She stole things." When Mrs. Pearson stopped talking, she turned away quickly, blinking. She was short but big, round and creased, and her legs weren't long enough: she practically toppled into her chair, throwing herself backwards at the cushions, and when she came to rest, her legs stuck out awkwardly as if they could not bend, and would not reach the floor anyway.

Better than the last one.

Paul hadn't talked much about past employees, just said that it wasn't an easy job to fill and that they'd gone through several people. Paul was in his sixties, hefty around the middle, and fully grey. He had the southern lawyer look down pat, Frank thought. The office was panelled in dark wood, surroundings that oozed quiet, expensive legal confidence. From behind a broad, smooth airstrip of desk, Paul had said that his mother wasn't easy to deal with – but Frank shouldn't be worried: "She'll warm up to you quickly," Paul said, winking. "She's got a thing for men. Treats 'em more politely than women. Must be generational."

Frank didn't know what to say about that, but he could certainly use the money and the roof over his head. Sure, everything in the house was old and dark, and some of the furniture looked pretty frail – and there was a constant smell halfway between mold and dirty dishes – but he couldn't afford to be picky.

"They always steal," Mrs. Pearson said the next time she spoke. Frank wasn't really sure that she was talking to him as much as just going over familiar ground. "They steal the nice things. Only the nice things, the expensive things. One moment they're here, sitting on the shelf as pretty as can be. The next they're gone. And money. You have to keep your eyes open, because they steal money, too. From an old lady, if you can believe that."

"Don't worry," Paul-the-lawyer said when Frank talked to him about it.

"She always thinks someone is stealing. Thing is, she's losing it a bit upstairs. She remembers stuff she used to have, can't remember that she doesn't still have it, says people stole it. We've had some bad apples, all right, but I wouldn't worry about it too much if I were you."

Paul laughed.

"I'd worry a lot more if she decided you might be a terrorist. Rush Limbaugh and the bunch have her all riled up, and you don't know what she'd do. And another thing – she's petrified about home invasions. Haven't been more than a handful, but if there's a door between you and her, you might want to knock – and speak respectful."

"She's not dangerous, is she?" Frank asked.

"Well, she's armed," Paul said jovially. "But she hasn't shot anyone yet."

It sounded like a joke – but that was before Frank heard the voices.

Frank had a room on the second floor of the house. It was a split-level, the kind of house where all the practical mechanical pieces – the washer, the dryer, the big chest-freezer with its constant steady hum – were in the basement. The trees outside were too big and too rarely trimmed, so that the inside of the house was cool and dark even in summer. Most of the furniture looked out of place – a dark wooden curio cabinet with curved glass, for example, that looked like it belonged in a Victorian home, and a huge mahogany dining room table that was way too large for the dining room. All of it looked as if it belonged in a bigger, older house – and that's where it had been, Mrs. Pearson explained.

"Stairs, that's the problem," she said, slipping her feet into soft pink bedroom slippers that would be crammed to capacity when her feet had finished swelling up by the early afternoon. "I would have been happy to stay in the old house if it wasn't for the stairs. One or two trips up and down, and I'd be done for the day. Anyway, Paul wanted to sell it, said it was cheaper and I'd be safer here, and he was willing to handle everything. He told me we got a very good price. He handles all the financial stuff, and without a word of complaint. He's a lovely boy."

Frank couldn't help think how much she reminded him of his own mother – perhaps it was the way she stuck her chin right up and out at him when she was making a point, as if the very intensity of her belief leant weight to her argument. Or perhaps it was the solid way her feet would thud down the hall towards the kitchen, purpose in every step.

Footsteps weren't the only thing he heard.

The split-level that Paul had bought for his mother meant Frank shared a wall – a thin, modern, hollow gyprock wall – with Mrs. Pearson's bedroom, and she was close to deaf in one ear, so he heard the voices on the very first night.

It was after one when he woke up the first time.

"America needs to know who she can trust," one voice said, and addled by sleep, Frank felt he almost had to agree – America did need to know who she could trust.

Then the same voice told him that public opinion polls showed Americans would be happier and sleep sounder knowing Muslims – and only Muslims – had gone through some sort of registration process.

By then, Frank was fully awake – the voice sounded angry, American talk radio seeping through the wall the way it was starting to creep across the Canadian border.

It wasn't easy to hear clearly through the gyprock, but the harder he listened, the more words he could make out. "Liberal lawyers," the voice hissed quietly. "Snakes, all of them." Frank got out of bed and pressed his ear to the wall, wondering all the while what Mrs. Pearson would make of it if she decided to burst in, and found him there, nearly naked, his face against her wall.

And that was Frank's introduction to American talk radio.

Some nights, Mrs. Pearson would work her way through the entire radio dial, sampling fuzzy and distant stations that only occasionally made the trip, trying to find the show that best approximated her own views. Sometimes, it took several tries. Michael Savage, G. Gordon Liddy – Frank learned new names almost every night.

And the pieces he heard were sometimes startling.

"Every stinking, rotten left-winger in this country … is a greater threat to your freedom than al-Qaida…."

"It's idiots like you who cause this country to go up in flames…."

"… moron, moron, moron…"

Frank was reminded of tapes he had heard about once, from a company that claimed you could learn Spanish just by running their tapes all night long.

Some sort of osmotic linguistics, he thought, where you soaked up a language the way roots soak up water.

"I think it's all going right into her head," Paul confided to Frank one afternoon in the dining room of the house. "She was once a dyed-in-the wool Trudeau Liberal, if you can believe that, but not any more. Worse the last few years, after she started on the talk radio from the States – seems to get nastier every week, and it just drags her along with it. You know, like you are what you eat. Now she says even the conservatives are too easy on criminals, and wonders why we ever got rid of hanging. If a teenager steals a bag of her groceries, she might well finish him off herself. I'm just glad we have handgun laws."

Paul laughed. Frank wasn't so sure that it was a laughing matter: after working there for just a few weeks, it already seemed to him that Mrs. Pearson was always agitated on the mornings after he heard the radio. It might just be the fact she hadn't slept well, he reminded himself.

He had even raised it with her, as delicately as he thought he could.

"You listen to some pretty opinionated folks on the radio, Mrs. Pearson," he had said one morning, passing her a cup of coffee. She was cooking them both scrambled eggs – two days in, she had told him he didn't really cook very well, and it would be better for both of them if she just went ahead and did it herself.

"You can hear my radio?" Mrs. Pearson seemed surprised. "I can barely hear it myself. Nothing to worry about there – that's just talk."

"But pretty extreme talk, Mrs. Pearson. When you're talking about taking away someone's civil rights because they belong to a minority group…"

"Well, they should have thought about those civil rights when they were crashing airplanes into those buildings and all." Mrs. Pearson set her jaw in a firm, straight line. "Fact is, we all have to be more careful, more willing to take things into our own hands. We used to be safe in our own country – we used to be safe in our own houses. Not now."

Frank recounted the conversation to Mrs. Pearson's son the next time Paul had come over, but he hadn't seemed that concerned.

"I don't think you have to worry too much, Frank. Taking things into her own hands? Heck, those hands can't even open a jam jar by themselves," Paul had said.

"They can fire a shotgun," Frank answered.

Frank had found the gun while he was vacuuming Mrs. Pearson's room – well, actually the nozzle of the vacuum had found it, when he was cleaning blindly under Mrs. Pearson's bed. He had looked, dropped the vacuum, and had headed for the phone to call Paul to ask what he should do about it. But Paul's secretary said he was meeting a client, and before Frank heard back, the gun had disappeared.

Frank wasn't about to dig around looking for it.

"That shotgun has to be fifty years old," Paul said. He was standing in front of the china cabinet – Frank noticed he was handling one of a set of small jade sculptures.

"And she's only ever fired it once, years ago – heard burglars in the kitchen of the old house, took out a patch of screen door the size of your head and shredded a bunch of branches on the lilac. Left a bruise on her shoulder the size of a dishpan. I don't think she'll be doing that again in a hurry." Paul closed the cupboard, and slipped his closed hand into his jacket pocket.

"Besides, if she pulls the trigger, the old thing's more likely to explode than shoot anything."

Thinking about the conversation later, Frank realized that while Paul was talking to him, something else was happening right there in front of his eyes. It was as if two different movies were playing at the same time – there was what Paul's voice was saying, and what his hands were doing. And once Paul had left and the house was quiet, Frank thought he understood.

But he would have to check to be sure.

Frank walked through the kitchen to the dining room, stopped in front of the curio cabinet and turned the little brass key. The two glass doors opened easily, and Frank began looking through the figurines, moving the ones in front out of the way so that he could be sure.

"Hands out of that cupboard, buddy-boy," Mrs. Pearson said. She was close up behind him, close enough that he could hear the click of her teeth when her mouth closed at the end of the sentence.

Frank froze.

"Mrs. Pearson, there used to be three jade figures here – but they're gone," Frank said, taking his hands away from the shelves slowly.

"Maybe they're in your pockets," Mrs. Pearson said. "Do you think we should check?"

Frank turned around slowly, his hands open in front of him. Mrs. Pearson was holding the wicked-looking shotgun, small gauge and bolt-action, but still big enough to seriously damage whatever she was shooting at. "Head-sized": Paul's words about the hole in the screen door swam through Frank's head unbidden.

"You can check if you like," Frank said carefully, looking hard at Mrs. Pearson's face. "But I think you should really be checking Paul's pockets."

He paused.

"And I think you know that, too."

Mrs. Pearson seemed to shrink right in front of him, and the end of the shotgun's barrel shook. Then she lowered the gun, so that it was pointing at his knees instead of his chest.

"You know it and I know it," Mrs. Pearson said slowly. Frank was surprised by how different her voice was, and by how her face had changed – as if, for weeks, he had been talking to a constructed and sometimes deliberately confused character, and now suddenly, he was faced with the real person.

"But no one else is going to know," she said, "and eventually, when enough stuff goes, I'll have to blame it on you, and you'll be gone, too. You're living on borrowed time, Frankie, borrowed time."

Frank looked at Mrs. Pearson, at the way her mouth set in a thin line so that she had almost no lips at all. The corners of her eyes pulled downwards, and

Frank could read in her face how deep the disappointment actually reached.

"Paul can't have a clue that I know," Mrs. Pearson said, resting the butt of the shotgun on the floor and pulling a chair out from the dining room table. She sat down – Frank closed the doors on the cabinet, but stayed standing where he was.

"I liked those jades," Mrs. Pearson said. "My husband brought them back to me when the boys were small and he had to travel so much. The insurance said they were worth $10,000 when we had the appraisals done, but that never really meant much to me."

She put the gun across the table and looked up at him.

"He's got big dreams and only a small law practice, and he's already been caught once dipping into the trust funds. Explained it away as some kind of misunderstanding, but the law society watches him pretty close. Every now and then, he's got to put a little something back. And there aren't many places for him to get it – he certainly can't ask me. Not and still live with himself."

"What are you saying – that he steals from you and you've both agreed to blame it on the help?"

"You're not listening, Frank. We haven't agreed on anything. He steals from me, and I blame it on the help so I don't have to blame it on him." She shook her head, eyes downcast, but then she turned and looked straight at Frank, her eyes as hard as beads.

"It's small things – valuable, yes, but he could just put me in a nursing home and have it all, and there's nothing I could do about it." She shrugged. "Sometimes, there's what you choose to know, and what's really true.

"You don't have children, Frank. If you did, you might understand. You make them and raise them, and everything they do is something you did right or wrong. They get in a fight in school, and maybe you were too strict or maybe you weren't strict enough," she said. "You're always doing something wrong, and you never know which one's actually going to leave a permanent mark."

She shook her head.

"He's old enough to be closing in on retirement, and he still needs to look good in my eyes. That's one good reason to get married, Frank. One good reason. So that you've at least got the chance to be close enough to someone to think you can be completely honest with them.

"Children are hopes and lies. Hopes for them, and a bunch of time spent lying to yourself."

And after that, they didn't talk about the theft again. One Mrs. Pearson – the straight, direct woman – vanished, and the other one reappeared: the polite, sometimes-confused woman with the right-wing chip on her shoulder. Frank began to wonder if Paul wasn't partially right, if the old woman wasn't losing something upstairs, after all.

At first, the memory hung unspoken in the air between them every day. But with each day, it was like it had drifted a little further out to sea.

And at night, the voices were getting louder and louder.

Frank thought Mrs. Pearson was probably having trouble sleeping, but so was he. The voices sometimes wove themselves into his dreams, and he found that increasingly disturbing.

One night, he dreamt he was at the scene of a terrorist bombing. It had the surreal feel that news coverage of explosions sometimes has: a building ripped cleanly in half by a bomb, so that you could look inside and see individual desks still set up on the edge of a precipice, with coffee cups and papers spread out as if the occupants had just gone to the bathroom. As if, at any moment, they would come right back and sit down again, getting on with their interrupted day. Frank was digging in the rubble, covered head to toe in dust, trying to find people he couldn't see, but could hear, calling for help. And then he looked at his hands and saw that his skin was brown, and he realized the other rescuers were looking at him. And then they started chasing him. And then, they had knives and guns in their hands.

He woke up drenched in sweat. Next door, he could hear someone bellowing from the radio.

"And the Democrats will just be standing by when they walk into your house or blow up city hall. They've cut defence spending until…"

Frank closed his eyes again. Sleep was slow in coming.

The next morning, he sat down at the table and wrapped his hands around the warmth of his coffee cup, determined to try and talk sensibly with Mrs. Pearson.

"They're just inventing enemies, Mrs. Pearson. Making up a threat because it suits their ends, which is getting the right people back in office."

"Invented enemies didn't blow up the twin towers," Mrs. Pearson said primly.

"American foreign policy started the…"

She interrupted him, waving her hands dismissively.

"We're bringing them democracy, Frank."

And night after night, the voices continued to whisper their fractured sweet nothings into Frank's ears while he tried to sleep.

Until Thursday.

Thursday, Mrs. Pearson was quieter than usual. Quieter, after Paul came by to visit and two Dorset soapstone carvings left with him, jogging heavily in his jacket pockets with each step. Mrs. Pearson said wistfully that she had owned the walrus of the pair for more than sixty years, and that its absence would "leave a little hole in my heart."

She went to bed early, and Frank took the opportunity to do the same. About one a.m., Mrs. Pearson turned her radio on, and the house filled with soft and angry words.

Around three in the morning, Frank suddenly thought he heard the front door open with a slow, drawn-out squeak. And then he was fully awake.

"You rat bastard terrorist," Mrs. Pearson shouted from the other end of the house, and then the shooting started. Frank heard two quick blasts, and then another.

By then, Frank was on the floor next to his bed, wondering who Mrs. Pearson had shot. He stayed there for a moment and then crept down the short hallway towards the living room.

The front door was wide open, and the living room was full of grey-blue gunpowder smoke. Frank saw Mrs. Pearson sitting in an armchair in the corner of the room, the shotgun between her knees.

Up over the front door, there were two gaping holes in the gyprock. Frank would remember thinking she must have had the choke cranked down tight on the shotgun, because all the pellets had stayed tight together, making the smallest holes possible. If she'd hit someone, he thought, she'd leave a hole the size of a grapefruit. A chair he knew she had never liked was blown apart, vomiting stuffing and springs. It looked like it had been shot at very close range.

The air was sharp and sulphurous, and he wasn't sure what Mrs. Pearson could see, settled in the dark corner like a chubby spider in a web, but he wasn't taking any chances.

"It's me, Mrs. Pearson — it's me, Frank," he called, loud enough to be sure she heard.

"I like you, Frank," Mrs. Pearson said distractedly, "so it will be all right."

She leaned back in the chair, and both of them could hear the sound of sirens in the distance, growing louder as they rapidly approached the house.

"You should put the gun down, Mrs. Pearson, before the police get here. You wouldn't want to get yourself shot."

"We'd better get our stories straight here, too, Frank."

The sentence came out hard, like a command. Frank could imagine the way her face would be set in straight lines, over there in the dark, the way her face would bulge outwards hard below the cheekbones when she set her jaw.

"Let's say there were two of them, all in black, and they sounded like foreigners. They *were* foreigners, actually," Mrs. Pearson said. "And they were out here for a while, digging around, because we heard them. They got a bag of stuff, we don't know really what. And then I scared them off."

Mrs. Pearson opened the bolt of the shotgun, and he heard the click as she pressed in a fresh shell. Then she bent over and set the gun down on the floor.

She looked up at Frank, and he thought that she was smiling.

"My goodness," she said, clapping her hands against the side of her face in mock dismay. "It will take ages to figure out everything they've taken. We'll be finding stuff missing for months."

"There weren't any..." Frank started.

Then Mrs. Pearson reached out one hand towards Frank, who was still standing just inside the living room door, confused, and held a finger in front of his lips, a single, wrinkled, gently shaking finger. He could see her face more clearly now, and her words came slowly.

"Frank, sometimes it's what you choose to know," she said as she pulled her hands back towards herself, palms upward. "Let's just say I've bought you and me a little more time."

Better Than This

WATCHING FROM THE WINDOW IN THE kitchen, Margaret saw the car as it slowed down on the road, saw it as the turn signal came on. Her hands were flat against the front of her jeans, the palms unconsciously rubbing up and down along her thighs.

Two people in the car, and Margaret Hennessey knew who they were – Alicia and Dan, the Forrestals, reservations for the next two days – and she had already tried out their first names, speaking them softly in front of the bathroom mirror and watching the way her own lips moved.

Margaret's farmhouse was tucked back into the side of a forested hill, triangular wedges of spruce running upwards and surrounded by the brighter greens of birches and maple, and out in front of the house, there was a long, close-cropped field running down to the road. It was midsummer, and outside the grass was already mostly brown, dead straw, a nest of earwigs curling around each other under the unused child's slide. The front door was open in that way that suggested hot, airless, still nights – open as if trying to invite in any possible current of air. Two dogs – big, black dogs lying in the shade cast by the corner of the house with their muzzles on their front paws, also watched the car stop at the top of the long gravel drive from the road.

Dan got out of the car quickly and came around the hood, around to Alicia's side of the car even before she had her door fully open.

The dogs were up and at the end of their chains in an instant, barking furiously, their collars pulled deep into their necks, hanging half-leaping forward and gasping as if the chain could break at any moment and let them hurl forwards. Margaret strode down the hall and out the front door quickly, snapping a dish-cloth at the barking dogs.

"Down!" she said sharply, turning to the couple. "Don't mind them. More show than anything else. They'll quiet."

She could see the Forrestals were shaken, and it made her want to reach out to protect them – the bare, almost-empty look that flashed across both their faces, the way they edged closer together and Alicia reached out and took Dan's hand.

The couple stayed that way even after the dogs had flopped back down in the dust, panting. They were meekly holding hands as they walked into the house behind Margaret. Newly married, Margaret thought as the couple followed her inside, their faces still soft and unformed. The thought made her smile, remembering.

Through the front door, it was possible to look in and see all the way up the stairs. The door was on the left side of the house, a bay window on the right, and the front of the house – wood shingles – was thick with old white paint, coat after coat. The old windows were covered with aluminum storms, the aluminum weathered and grey. Over the second floor, a high, peaked roof of green asphalt shingles, the pitch of the roof too steep to climb or to even stand on.

Deep in the Annapolis Valley, Nova Scotian apple country, the farm was boxed in on both sides by long rows of apple trees, tended in that careful way that makes each tree look hobbled – the top suckers clipped away carefully every year, so the tree stays low and fans out strong, crabbed lower branches. Easier for the pickers in the fall when the apples get heavy and bright red, but a kind of trimming that leaves their silhouettes low-shouldered and hunched, branches reaching for the ground.

The trees also had a way of standing like a fence, like tired sentries with grass growing up between their feet, regimented lines that stood between each orchard and the next running down the length of the valley. The farms were spread out along both sides of the road, but not across from each other – their presence assumed, rather than seen. There were neighbours who were near enough to call for help – and ready, too, ready the way they had all been when they rushed to the big dairy barn near Gasperaux as it burned hot and fast early on a spring morning, the cattle all lowing at first, and then, awfully, all silent – but also far enough away that a passing wave of the hand on the way down the road counted as socializing. Her husband Jack's family was even nearby, the closest geographically a quiet brother named David who lived up behind them on North Mountain in a trailer on family land. But even the family kept to themselves.

It made the white farmhouse with the perfect trim like a kind of gingerbread prison.

It left her wanting to go anywhere, even to get out to the crumbling shoreline club at Evangeline Beach – Margaret loved even the idea of that, the thought of seeing anyone else she knew, the idea of a night among people, any other people. She seized every chance, even going to the Top Hat in New Minas with Jack when the strippers ("the peelers," he called them) came to town. Just to be out – to drink rye and to laugh and to sparkle and flirt – Margaret could remember a time when she did just that, before they were married, when they would wake up beside each other and wonder just how the hell the car had gotten back into the driveway, and which one of them had actually been driving.

When the sheets were a knotted turmoil, when the nights were panting and desperate and eager, and there was a reason to want to be far away from everyone.

But things settled. Settled onto a straighter road, she thought, and then right down into the wheel ruts.

She was better than this – she told herself that, over and over again.

Better than this, and she should never have wound up here in the first place, married to an orchard and a tank-sprayer, married to a man who was flat on his back, asleep on the couch at nine o'clock almost every night, a short row of Alpine beer cans next to him on the carpet.

In her mind, they were supposed to work the place together, and she saw herself striding down between the rows of trees in something as romantic as a gingham dress, the sleeves pulled up past the elbows of her long arms, the laundry flapping out behind her on the line like signal flags. In her mind, it was supposed to have been noble and romantic, the sort of nobility that comes from working together to downright pull success right out of the ground with your bare hands.

And there had been a clear shot at that, at least at first. She had worked the orchards, until it became obvious that the only time Jack actually needed help was at the harvest, and then there were plenty of migrant pickers to hire for that.

"Look," Jack had said, working on the tractor, wiping oil from his hands and turning towards her. "I drive better than you, and there's really only driving. The pickers'll stack the bushels."

"But I want to help," Margaret had said.

"Well, then help by staying out of the way." He might not have meant it to feel like a slap.

The pickers came first for strawberries, then zucchini, then the cherries and plums. They came last for the apples, lots of apples, and for a few brief weeks the valley would be full of people twisting the fruit off stiff woody stems, and seeing how many bushels they could get paid for in a single, cold-breathed fall day.

She had even tried winter logging, up on the long hill, cutting hardwood to sell cut into junks, and for big softwood for the mill, but she just wasn't strong enough to keep up, to keep pressing the big sawlogs chest-high up into the rick behind the tractor. And then Jack had gotten Bill Preston from down the road, a quiet bull of a man, and Bill didn't even have to wait for Jack to put down the saw: he could lift the big, snow-covered eight-foot lengths into the rick all by himself almost every time.

Then she and Jack had tried miniature horses, briefly and expensively, ending up worse off than when they had started. Then they bred black Labrador retrievers. That had all died off – and pretty quickly, too, as quickly as the last two litters of puppies when the power failed for two days in a March ice storm, their mothers disturbed and wandering away from the puppies, walking out of the kennels and around the dog runs, the dogs shaken by the noise of the clattering, ice-covered trees.

Soon there was just the house, the occasional liberation of shopping for groceries. The nights were too quiet, and the days were worse.

The tourist cabins had been one last desperate throw of the dice – Jack had built them without even complaining about the cost of the materials. Three small cabins in a line down one side of the field towards the road, but they had been her idea, and then suddenly, her responsibility, too. There was something about the cabins, about the way they all lined up evenly below the house. It was all right, Margaret thought, when there were people staying there, when there would be cars or minivans in the three narrow driveways, when there were lights on at night. Otherwise, they looked oddly out of place, even though Jack had planted them as evenly as if they had been three more trees in the orchard.

He had done the framing for the concrete, had put up the stud walls and the gyproc, talking all the while to his green-bubbled level, lips barely moving. She had plastered and picked out paint, hung wallpaper, put down the floors and finished the trim. And for a while, it was like they were working together – but only until the three low buildings were finished. They shouldered the box springs and mattresses in together, painted the outsides of each cottage, and one night they sat on the floor in the cabin furthest from the farmhouse, drinking beer. Margaret looked across at Jack, and for a fleeting moment saw a glimpse of the boy she had fallen in love with.

"It looks good," Margaret said, reaching out toward the newly-painted wall with one fingertip.

"This one could actually work," he said, grinning. "We should celebrate."

She was surprised how much she had missed his touch, how exquisitely good his hands felt on her bare hips – and she revelled in reuniting with her big, strong, eager boy.

But then, like a door slamming, things returned to normal, returned to worse than ever.

When winter came, he was out the door almost without speaking at seven in the morning, leaving the farmhouse as cold as it was when he got up. She would make her way down to the kitchen wrapped in a housecoat to light the kitchen stove, to try and coax some heat from newspaper and thin slivers of kindling. Once the fire was going, always a little smoke coming back into the room, she'd sit on a kitchen chair and draw her feet in up under her, under the edge of the housecoat, and wait until the metal of the stove started to warm the room and nibble away at the delicate frost flowers on the inside of the window glass. Then she would stand in the porch and smoke furiously, short, sharp breaths of cigarette smoke, hating every puff, absolutely unable to stop.

Spring, when it came, was a relief, even though the snow kept coming back – snow in April, again on the first of May, snow on Margaret's birthday, eight days deep into May when the first of the apple blossoms might appear in warmer years.

No one rented the cabins until the end of June, and even when they did, it was somehow disappointing: one evening, the yard in front of the cabins would be stuffed with kids and noise and the smoking barbecues, and the next, it would be empty again, as if someone had pulled the plug and all the noise had been sucked like water down the drain. They'd be gone, and Margaret would look out the window and imagine that the swings on the swing set were still moving back and forth, so sudden was the change. It felt like they had built a way station on the highway, less a destination than a place where visitors stopped on an urgent journey to someplace else.

July was slow, August was practically still. Then the Forrestals arrived.

She took their credit card and gave them the keys in the small office she had made out of a desktop in a narrow closet by the stairs, thinking it was funny how being alone so often could make you notice so much about other people. Like the way Alicia would take a half-step sideways towards Dan as a matter of course as soon as you spoke to either of them. To Margaret, it didn't seem that the Alicia was possessive, as much as it seemed she was sheltering behind the slender, dark Dan.

Alicia's eyebrows were so blond they were virtually invisible, and it gave her narrow face an almost permanent look of puzzled surprise. She was willowy in the way that makes you think of fine hands folded, protectively praying in front of someone's chest. Dan was a good counterpoint – not a big man, really, but solid and dark-whiskered, as if he had to shave twice a day. They were from Halifax, just over an hour's drive, out of town for the weekend.

Walking out to the middle cabin, Margaret hoped they wouldn't mind that the dishes didn't match, that the glasses and silverware were a collection of remnants scratched up and bought cheap at yard sales and church bazaars, that the magazines were year-old

Maclean's and decorating magazines with a thousand ideas for inexpensive quick-fixes.

The Forrestals drove down behind her slowly as she walked, making a short and formal procession, and there was a fleeting moment when she wondered what they thought of her legs. Just for a moment, really, a distracting thought as if a blackfly had buzzed too close to her ear. Then the engine of the car was off, and Dan was pulling luggage from the trunk and Alicia was opening the door.

"I can pack you a lunch tomorrow," Margaret said. "if you want to go exploring."

"That would be nice," Alicia nodded, and Margaret was only three strides back up the drive when she heard the door of the cabin close, and the snick of the doorknob turning inside, setting the lock.

In the morning, it was homemade white bread and roast chicken, heavy with mayonnaise and wrapped tight in Saran. No apples yet, but fleshy yellow plums, the kind that burst sweet and wet on your lips with the first bite. The fruit rich for only a few days, going past quickly when the skins turn transparent and the flesh goes soft.

Alicia came into the kitchen while Margaret was putting the picnic together, came in and leaned against the kitchen counter. Margaret noticed how slender her arms were, the way she crossed those arms carelessly so that it looked like her hands only met her elbows as an afterthought.

"Thanks," Alicia said quietly, as if the words took tremendous effort. "It's awfully nice of you."

"You and Dan should go down to Scott's Bay and look for agates," Margaret said, looking at her own hands as she spread the mayonnaise. "The wind's off the water, and you'll be cooler. Take a sweater, though, it can be foggy with the wind in this direction." She could imagine them on the beach, both in heavy sweaters, walking slowly along the angled gravel, watching for the bright quartzes, for the agates and amethyst and the brilliant orange crystals of zeelite. Margaret hadn't been there for years, but she could remember the narrow dirt road down to the beach, the way it ended just before the great grey dunes of small stones, the narrow, white-painted bridge, bowed up in the middle, that you walk across to get to the beach itself.

"Tides are fast there," Margaret said, and she could have sworn that Alicia jumped at the sound of her voice – no, not jumped, but started, perhaps, the way horses suddenly lurch away, jangled, big, smooth legs suddenly awkward and akimbo. Margaret had to resist the urge to reach out for her.

"Sorry?" Alicia said.

"The tides," Margaret said slowly. "The tides are fast out there. So you have to be careful."

Margaret had a basket she had been saving for a picnic, a basket she had never used, and she took it down from the top of the cupboards where it had always been. She put in the sandwiches and fruit, and passed it to Alicia, and for a moment Margaret felt the cool smooth skin of Alicia's fingers.

"We'll do that," Alicia said, and even after the couple had left, Margaret could see the map she had drawn for them in her head, could imagine them driving down through Wolfville, through Canning, down to where the road began to bend around along the ocean because it had no other choice. In under the big elms that Dutch elm disease hadn't found yet, out past the low, slow brooks where the ducks worked the muddy water, their tailfeathers upright as they dipped, head down.

Sitting in the kitchen, she could picture the postcard-perfection of it: the fishing boats at the ends of their lead-lines, Cape Islanders all, settled hull-down into the deep red Minas Basin mud. Abandoned by the tide, waiting calmly for its resurrection. The deep green blades of dune grass, the fine-gravel beach that ran away at such a discrete angle that it looked as if it was actually level, so close to flat that the tide boiled in low and fast like one long, never-breaking shallow wave.

Margaret could imagine the rattle of the road gravel, thrown up under the car from the dirt road, the semaphore of pings and clangs, that rare and wonderful disordered song. And she could remember how long it had been since she had been on that road, one elbow out the window in the baking sun, the hot summer vinyl seat burning the backs of her thighs, a delta of dust growing out behind the car.

Then suddenly Alicia and Dan would take a left up the hill past the shotgun tarpaper shacks, past the mobile homes and the abandoned pickup trucks, onto the marginal ground where the orchards were scabby and stunted, short of sun. Up through where the brooks had cut deep valleys in the soft red sand-stone, where the maples would change in great flam-ing fury in the fall, where, for a few short weeks, the leaves would be almost too bright to look at. She could imagine them holding each other's hands, could imagine someone holding her hand.

Then suddenly they would be thrown out into the open, heading along the spine of the hill towards Scott's Bay. A row of abandoned, sheered-off wharf pilings, heading out into the sea below the tide line, their genesis forgotten.

No wonder in it at all, there on the narrow grey-black strip of asphalt through the head-high alders, no wonder save for the sudden discovery of the huge broad grey crescent of beach stone. No wonder except for the fact that, on hands and knees, the gravel is filled with scores of semi-precious stones, and occasionally, very occasionally, the strangely milky swirl of a lonely teardrop opal.

Alicia brought the basket back empty, and smiled.

"Thanks," she said. "The beach was wonderful."

But this was nothing Margaret didn't already know.

Later, when it began to get dark, the heat began to fall off the day. It fell away in sheets with the setting sun: one moment, as heavy and oppressive and damp as sweat; the next, the cool of sudden evening wind, gathering and racing out from under the trees where it had been sheltering, biding time.

Margaret sat on the steps of the back porch, feet apart, watching the sky wash through orange to black. She shook a cigarette out of the pack, but this one she smoked slowly, drawing the smoke in and holding it for a moment before exhaling.

It was almost completely dark when the door to the Forrestal cabin opened. She watched, still smoking, as Dan came out on the porch and stretched. She inhaled, saw him stop and stare towards her, towards the suddenly-bright coal at the end of her cigarette. He started walking towards her, hands in his pockets.

"It's beautiful here," he said when he reached the bottom of the steps. He pointed towards the cigarette. "Got another?" Margaret nodded, knowing Dan could barely see her in the gloom. She shook out a cigarette, passed it to him, and reached over with hers. He lit his and sat on the steps. Margaret leaned forward and rested her forearms on her knees. They sat quietly for a few moments.

"Don't smoke that much anymore," Dan said. "Especially in front of Alicia."

"She knows anyway," Margaret said, knowing the way Jack would sometimes wrinkle up his forehead and nose when he came into the kitchen, even though she always smoked outside.

"Yeah, well, she pretends she doesn't. And I pretend I don't smoke," he said. "It's a relationship built on mutual denial."

They sat quietly, looking across the stubbled grass as car headlights swept down the road. The night insects were singing, and from the standing water behind the house, there were the high trilling peeps of small green frogs.

"It's hard not to love it here," Dan said, breathing out smoke. The air was so still that it seemed to hum, to vibrate in the darkness.

"Can't stand it here any more," Margaret said. "Even quiet can crush you."

"I can't believe that," Dan said. "I can't believe that you don't like it. I would."

"Yeah, well, then I'll pretend I do. And you can pretend to believe me, and we can build something mutual on that," Margaret said.

Margaret thought she saw the white flash of his teeth against his face for a moment, but in the dark she wasn't sure. He flicked the cigarette away, and they watched its ember tumble end over end away onto the driveway. Her cigarette landed along the edge of the grass.

She watched hers smouldering in the short grass, and knew she'd be the one to come out and collect both of the cold, charred filters in the early morning.

"Gotta get back," Dan said, standing up and hitching his jeans up around his hips. She watched him walk away.

She stayed outside until the dew suddenly fell, until the night was cooler and there were tiny water droplets all over the painted steps, and the whole time the cars kept swinging by the gentle curve in the road out in front of her, kept swinging by, heading for somewhere more interesting.

Margaret could see them through the yellow-lit windows of their cabin, and Dan was standing behind her, behind Alicia, with his arms around her waist.

Then his hands were under her shirt and Alicia was leaning back, pushing against him and Margaret looked away again, down towards the road.

The Forrestals left the next morning around eleven, and Margaret left the keys and the credit card slip on the table, as if they might change their minds. The dew was already long gone, the air already heavy again.

And Jack was on the tractor, hauling the big mower up and down the long field between the house and the road, the chaff and dust rising in a cloud behind him. Looking out the kitchen window, she could only see his back and the back of his head, and the deep, dusty vee of sweat down the middle of the back of his T-shirt as he drove away from her. His head didn't move, as if he were completely consumed with the task at hand, as if he could not imagine that there was anything on earth, not one single thing anywhere, beyond grass and hoppers and dust.

Alicia gave an offhand wave as the car pulled around the corner of the house and headed down the driveway. Dan was looking straight ahead at the road, and he didn't turn his head, not even once. Margaret would have noticed if he had.

"Oh," she moaned to the blind pane of kitchen window glass, to the rooster-tail of roadway dust settling behind the car as it pulled away. "Oh." And Margaret put her forehead against the glass and cried.

Housekeeping

IAN KINLEY ARRIVED AT THE SEASHELL MOTEL in a taxi, and that was strange enough.

Settled down on the side of a highway outside Halifax, Nova Scotia, the Seashell was the kind of crumbling motel where you drove in one night, and drove out the next morning.

And that was the second strange thing: Ian wasn't leaving in the morning.

When the clerk asked him "Just tonight?" Ian answered "We'll see," all the time tapping the edge of his credit card impatiently on the counter.

"Licence number?"

"Nope. No car."

"Bags?"

"Just this," and Ian held up a small brown fabric suitcase.

"Unit 14," the desk clerk said. The new guest was a small man, maybe in his seventies, with a thin, deeply wrinkled face and white hair. He was wearing a brown jacket and dress pants, much more formal than most guests, who favoured T-shirts, jeans and baseball caps.

Ian walked slowly to his unit, stopping occasionally to breathe deeply and painfully. His doctor had said it was only pleurisy, but Ian thought of it — repeatedly — as the last straw. The pace gave him a chance to look at the units carefully. Each one was the same. Except for the corner units, they shared common walls on both sides, and uniform, greying white stucco on the front. Each had two rectangular windows — one large, one small — underlined with once-jaunty window boxes full of dead or dying flowers. The geraniums were struggling — the pansies had long since died of thirst. There was a parking space in front of each one, with a white number painted on the pavement.

Ian watched the numbers as he walked: eleven, twelve, fourteen. He always found that odd: it was like buildings where there was no thirteenth floor, where the elevator buttons left out one odd number as they climbed. Perhaps the idea was that superstition would make them hard to rent, he thought. But he was pragmatic enough about that: he'd be fine staying in thirteen, whatever they decided to call it.

Inside, the room was like any other — two queen-sized beds with busily patterned bedspreads designed to hide stains, a television with the remote control laid squarely in front of it. He'd turned down the minibar key. He laid his suitcase on the bed near the window, and walked into the bathroom, flicking on the light. The bathroom, he knew, would back onto another bathroom in the suite next door – another way to save a little money on construction.

Ian looked at himself in the big bathroom mirror, trying to reconcile the person looking back at him with the picture he had of himself. The man in the mirror shook his head resignedly. Ian walked back to the bed and opened the suitcase. Socks, underwear, one clean shirt. He picked up two handfuls of pill bottles, his razor and toothbrush, and went back to the bathroom. He lined the bottles up in front of the glass, next to the two clean, upside-down water glasses.

Doctors like to have you out of their office, he thought. They like to think they've done the right thing, but they also like to be rid of you, rid of your nagging complaints. Old age complaints, he thought, regularly mitigated but never cured.

If you're in your seventies, just go in and tell them you're having trouble sleeping, and they'll get the prescription pad out right away.

Ian looked at the five bottles of pills sitting next to each other. Four to keep me alive, he thought, and one to do something quite different. One to keep his blood thin, one to keep his blood pressure down, another for angina, a fourth, antibiotics for his lungs. And the sleeping pills.

Ian had never had trouble sleeping – nightmares, yes, but sleep had always been like falling off a bridge. A few seconds to ponder the day before you hit the black water of sleep hard. But he had forty sleeping pills now, big red and yellow capsules, each one, the doctor had assured him "strong enough to put a horse to sleep."

He left the bathroom, pulled the curtains open.

His room looked out on the parking lot, and across the road, a lobster pound where the overnight refrigerated trucks sat, engines running, waiting for morning and loads of crustaceans. Right in front of his unit in the empty parking space was a huge stain of transmission fluid. Later, when it rained, the pavement there would bead up with shiny, oil-topped drops, each with its own twirling, circling rainbow. The drops dried last, long after the rest of the asphalt had lightened.

Ian met Rosie the afternoon he checked in: he was coming out the door of his unit while she was coming in, the bulky housekeeping cart blocking most of the sidewalk.

Rosie Kirk had dark eyebrows that knotted together constantly, as if she were overwhelmingly concerned. They were at odds with the rest of her wide, open face – Ian noticed that she always smiled when she met someone, as if she felt she owed them a pleasant response. Big across the shoulders, she looked more like a softball player than anything else, and a cheerful one at that. But the eyebrows gave her away, put the lie to the smile.

"Just checking to see if everything's all right," Rosie said brightly. Ian had yet to even pull back the covers on the bed to see what the pillows were like.

If I dropped my things back in the suitcase, he thought, there'd be no sign I'd been here at all. But that's the way it is with hotels; check in, check out, and vanish without a trace.

"It's fine," Ian said, smiling back at Rosie. "All I really need."

At the same time, he wished he hadn't run into the woman. It was too much to put a face to her – he couldn't help imagining, now, what it would be like when Rosie came into the room afterwards. But that was another day, and Ian suddenly realized how hungry he was.

OUTSIDE THE MOTEL, he set off down the road, walking on the gravel shoulder, teetering slightly. The ditches were alight with flowers – there were still wild strawberries, he saw, even though he didn't bend down to pick any. Wild strawberries and the bright green of raspberry canes. The tangled strands of wild roses, the flowers still tightly-furled and pink-tipped. Trash in the ditch, too, and Ian couldn't help but try to put together a sort of history for each piece. All stories, he thought, from the candy wrapper some child had dropped out of a car window, to the ripped condom package, its torn edge fluttering in the breeze, to the way the beige timothy grass seeds were coming away from their stalks. That was the one part he regretted: such a waste to collect so much information, so much experience, only to have it turn off like a light bulb.

Sure, the practical stuff carried on – he knew there wasn't anyone who needed to hear from him about how to wire a three-phase electrical plug, or what kind of varnish was right for trim. But there had to be some use for and some way to share the other stuff: the knowledge that the searing part of love can be fleeting, and should be carefully savoured for as long as possible; that wine tastes different in the dark; that every chance you take is electric in its own way, and that its charged tingle is far from unpleasant.

He was at his destination already. In front of him was the sign for the restaurant, an oval sign lined all around with light bulbs: *Mae's*. It was a small restaurant with booths and matronly waitresses in white uniforms, a familiar kind of spot, and Ian realized you could actually see the ocean from most of the tables.

He had a simple meal, clam chowder and a dinner roll. The roll was warm – Ian used both of the small plastic containers of butter, and didn't stop to think about it. He wiped the last of the chowder up with the roll, and felt a great release from doing exactly what he wanted. Then he sat quietly with his coffee – two cream, one sugar – and looked out the restaurant's big windows, across the train tracks and out over the short-chopped waves of Bedford Basin. There was a container ship moored there, swinging on its anchors and stacked high with orange and blue containers. Ian imagined where the big metal containers were going, tried to guess what it was they held.

Leaning back in the cushioned booth, he couldn't remember being more comfortable. I'll wait one more day, he thought. One more day. Nothing wrong with eating clam chowder two days in a row.

Soon, it was five days in a row, and the staff was saying they couldn't remember the last time a guest had stayed so long. Ian was almost a fixture by then, walking down the road on rainy days, sitting by the pool when it was sunny. He had convinced the taxi company to deliver beer right to his unit, the driver always careful to look both ways, up and down the highway, before getting out of the taxi with the six-pack.

By Wednesday, six days and counting, it looked like he might not ever leave.

That afternoon, in the early July heat, the desk-clerk – his real name was Doug, but by then Ian knew everyone called him Bud – was swinging a hockey stick through the grass behind the motel, taking the heads off dandelions and knocking them away across the grass. Bumblebees were droning slowly in circles, and Bud was taking his time. It was two o'clock in the afternoon, and Bud knew no one would be checking in for hours – it would be five o'clock at the earliest when the first of the exhausted all-day drivers would flop their chubby forearms down on the counter and tug wallets out of their too-tight jeans.

Ian watched the heat shimmer up off the pool deck, and reached into the box for another beer.

"You could put them in ice," Bud shouted over to him. "Ice machine's fixed."

"That's all right," Ian called back. "Don't mind them warm. Want one?"

"No, Mr. K.," Bud said, taking aim at another dandelion and winding the hockey stick back for another slapshot. "I'm working, remember?"

By then, Ian had realized that travellers stayed at the Seashell so they could get up with the sun for an early start on the road. The housekeeping staff often forgot to reset the clock radios after guests checked out, but no one complained. Five-thirty in the morning was always time to go.

Heavy trucks would overnight in the back lot, their drivers in the bar down the road until closing. There were campers looking for one night with a bathroom and shower before going back to roughing it, and pickup trucks loaded with furniture – almost always on the thirtieth of the month – their owners in the process of moving to new apartments. Those were the standard guests.

The Seashell was convenient, clean, cheap and on the way – but it was never going to be a holiday destination, despite the pool the owners had installed a few years earlier. The only swimmers in the pool were June bugs and flying ants, doing marathon backstrokes, supported by surface tension until they finally expired.

Ian's pool chair was the only one that was set up – a stack of folded chairs sat at the end of the pool nearest to the back of the motel, tied in place with frayed yellow nylon rope. The tops of the chairs were worn to a matte white from the weather. Ian could feel a slick of sweat forming where his body touched the vinyl straps of the chair.

For Ian, the warm beer held its own alchemy, and it fired its own set of memories, taking him back to the backyard behind his Halifax house. Just sitting on the porch, sipping beer, watching the evening fade away into the steady orange glow of the streetlights. Watching the peonies blossom, big fat buds that opened rich, and then bent face down, embarrassed. You had to be careful with peonies, Ian thought, too much damp early and the buds get fungus and die. He wondered how they were doing there without him.

It's only a cab ride away, he thought, but it could just as well be in another country. He walked through the checklist in his head. He'd turned the breakers off for the hot water heater so the electrical bill would be lower. Car cleaned out, locked and left in the drive-way. All of the garbage cans were emptied, the litter box cleaned, the big green bag out by the curb before he left. He had left a careful note right where they would find it, on the table inside the back door. He had even thought about bagging up his clothes for the Good Will, but had reconsidered. That seemed almost too carefully planned.

Better for them to have something to do to work through it all, he had thought at the time. He hoped someone would adopt Tip from the SPCA. He didn't like the idea of the cat being put down, but it was that or just leave him outside, and doing that seemed far more cruel. He'd told the workers that he was going into an old age home, that Tip was healthy and well behaved and friendly. He didn't tell them that Tip loved killing birds, and that Ian had once seen the cat, leaping, pick a robin clean out of the sky. After that, he had kept Tip inside the house for two weeks, feeling complicit.

Ian was proud of the house, even thinking about it now. He'd done a lot of work to make it just the way he wanted: whoever bought it would obviously do whatever they liked, but he preferred to think some parts – like the wainscoting – would live on, perhaps through a number of owners. He had pieced that wainscoting together carefully, not by any means a carpenter, but having the advantage of time. He'd measure a piece, put it up, and if it didn't look exactly right, he'd either take it down again, or stop until the next day, to see how the work looked to fresh eyes.

And that, Ian knew, was at the heart of why he was at the Seashell – at least, that had been the idea. He knew it might take his family a week or more to come and check on him – it was summer, and no matter how wonderful a companion Tip was, Ian had read too many newspaper stories about the nasty things pets did to their former owners. And he knew that part of him might lie there in the heat, ruining everything that he had ever done. At least at the Seashell, he knew someone would find him within a day or so.

He just hadn't expected that it would have to be Rosie.

She was working double shifts now, trying to make more money. He had thought of paying her a day's wages, and telling her to take her little boy to the beach. She had told him about herself, about her son,

John, while making the bed and pulling the bed-spread square. A little boy, brown hair, and blue eyes, a little too close to his father's looks for Rosie's liking.

"I guess I thought a youngster would make things better, make us a family, like," Rosie said. "Guess I was wrong."

"There are worse mistakes to make," Ian said. "At least you've got John."

Rosie's eyes agreed: she was using her chin to help fold fresh towels.

With Rosie working seven days a week, the four-year-old spent most days with his grandmother. Every day, Ian heard a little bit more: about how Rosie was just a few courses short of a college degree; about a house she had looked at renting; about how there was always something falling off her car.

"Wiper blades flew right off in the rain. First the passenger side, then mine." Rosie laughed. "Took right off, straight up, like they had wings. Driving down the highway at twenty 'cause I couldn't see anything." And as soon as she got new wipers, the wiper motor packed it in. Ian was amazed that she could still seem so cheerful.

"Find a new daycare?" Ian asked.

"Yup. Be easier if his father would just pay his share," she said. He could hear her lining up the toiletries, moving his shaving kit around on the counter. Then a pause.

"Lotta medicines in here, Mr. K," Rosie called from the bathroom.

Ian was flicking through channels on the television – he imagined her looking at the big brown bottle, the one where the level of the pills never changed, wondering why.

"Yeah, well, I'm old. You'll be old one day too, Rosie."

"I'm hoping I will be," Rosie said. "See ya tomorrow."

She closed the door to the room, and he heard the cart make its short trip to the next room, the wheels clattering on the rough pavement. The family from next door was gone – as usual, it had been just one night that they'd probably all soon forget, and it was the full clean, everything off the beds, the bathroom stripped right down to the towel racks. Folding the hide-a-bed back into the couch, all re-made and ready for the next family.

Ian had heard that there had been a fuss in the States about hotels saving money by not properly cleaning the rooms between guests. There was even a company marketing a sort of sleeping bag of sheets that you could slide into so you never even touched the hotel linen. He'd seen that on CNN and had just shaken his head – hotel linens were one of the best parts of a journey.

Rosie said there was never any problem changing a room over – that it was easier than cleaning one up where someone was staying an extra night.

"You just ball up all the sheets and try not to think about what might be on 'em. Better not to look sometimes," she said. "Towels too. Then you just start fresh and brand new."

Fresh and brand new – he had liked the sound of that. Tried it on the next morning, and walked a different way down the highway, strolling down a side road past big, new, expensive houses that got smaller as the road narrowed. Finally, just before the road ended, he came to a small house with a gabled roof, laundry hanging limp on the line. The yard was surrounded by a low fence and peonies stood all along the foundation on the sunny side of the house, the big balls of the buds hanging down slightly. It was the kind of house that he could imagine himself living in, or that might even suit Rosie and John. Anything's possible, he thought suddenly, why not? Why not all of them together? It wasn't impossible. Pierre Trudeau had conceived a daughter when he was seventy-two, for God's sake. Whoa, Ian thought just as quickly. You're way ahead of yourself here. Like Don Quixote, he thought. Like some lascivious old Don Quixote, riding to the rescue of a damsel who didn't really need rescuing, just an honest-to-God streak of good luck.

Walking back, Ian realized something else; it was the first time in months he had actually thought about some kind of future – the first time he had actually considered even having one. Too long in an empty house. His boys with their own families, his wife dead for ten years now, and Ian realized that he had always expected the little house to fill right back up all by itself. That he had been waiting for years for some different notion of family to appear and take up permanent residence.

Back in the motel unit, he sat on the end of his bed, thought for a moment about how the nape of Rosie's neck might feel. Then he shook himself, thinking this is stupid – the girl doesn't even call me by my first name.

He turned on the television, flung down the remote control.

And stopped.

A newsreader was talking about a missing man, and up in the corner of the television was a picture of himself – it was an old picture, from a family reunion highlighted by the spectacular food poisoning that had hit everyone who had eaten the potato salad. It was a picture that made Ian feel that he looked vaguely like an owl.

Then, the picture was bigger, filling the entire screen.

There was a knock on the door.

"Housekeeping," Rosie called, the master key scraping in the lock as she came in.

Ian scrambled for the unfamiliar remote control, but succeeding only in turning up the volume.

Rosie stood in the narrow hall, staring at the television, then staring at Ian, as a police telephone number unspooled across the bottom of the screen. The announcer's voice again, saying that the police wanted to hear from anyone who might have seen Ian Kinley, that the police felt there was a reason for concern.

"Well," she said, before going quiet for a moment.

Then, she said, "Well. Nobody needs to know that. We don't have to say anything, and they like you at Mae's, too. And maybe we can just get your beer delivered to the front desk."

Later, at the end of her shift, Rosie came back, without the cart but still dressed in her uniform.

She sat on the end of Ian's bed.

"I can't help it, this isn't right," she said. "I can't help thinking about your family, out there wondering where you are."

Ian tried to explain that he didn't really think it was like that, and the last thing he expected would be that they would be losing any sleep about him being alive somewhere. Told her about the note, and that, if they knew he was missing, they had to have found the two short pages of lined paper where he had outlined all his reasons. They were calling him missing on television, but truthfully, they had to be expecting that he was dead.

"They shouldn't be worried about me," Ian said. "They're just looking for the body, really."

"That's horrible too," Rosie said. "If you left a note for me, I'd want to know what happened to you. And I'm putting those pills down the toilet."

Ian rested his chin in his hands — this is all so much more complicated than it was supposed to be, he thought. It was a simple plan with no entanglements, and now it's all knots and no rope.

"A few more days, Rosie, that's all I want," Ian said finally. "Just a few more. Then you can call them."

Rosie wasn't convinced. "We'll see."

The next afternoon, Ian sat in the long recliner next to the pool, the sun shining on his white, knobby legs. Bud was away from the desk again, tired of waiting for guests who didn't arrive. He was scooping up the stray grass that had blown across the surface of the water when he mowed the lawn, along with picking out the occasional pool-bound ant struggling feebly.

Ian smiled. Bud shrugged, scooping another load of grass and bug bits from the blue water of the pool.

They'd figure it out eventually, figure out that he wasn't dead after all, and come and get him. They'd figure it out or else they'd just cancel his credit card, thinking someone had stolen it.

Until then, though, it was the simple wonder of clean sheets and restaurant food. And family. Bud had left the pool deck, and was unrolling a long hose, setting up a sprinkler to water the grass. Ian could hear the clattering wheels of Rosie's cart moving away down the pavement in front of the units. He imagined her legs, her uniform, the shampoo bottles rattling together on the cart. The look of deep concern that sometimes crossed her face like changing weather.

Nothing better than family, he thought. Nothing better at all.

Then he had another thought: some clam chowder perhaps, and later, I might go for a swim.

Acknowledgements

First of all, I know I'll have forgotten to mention many people who made this book possible, and who have my gratitude even if they aren't named individually. There are also several who deserve special recognition

In St. John's, my colleague and friend Pam Frampton read and edited many of the original drafts of these stories. They have been thoroughly edited by Leslie Vryenhoek, whose care, counsel and sheer hard work has made each and every one of these stories much, much better.

This collection could not have been completed without the good-natured and thorough support of my editor at Coteau, Edna Alford, who read the stories before they were even accepted for publication, and told me straight out to start thinking about how I would want a book cover to look. Her belief in this book has been nothing less than awe-inspiring. Joanne Gerber, who accepted the first story I published at

Grain, has been integral to bringing this work to the light of day.

This collection of stories would not have been possible without the time and dedication of the variety of people who have worked with me under the auspices of the Banff Centre's writing programs: David Bergen, Moira Farr, Ian Pearson and Rosemary Sullivan are just four of the people who deserve credit there. They, like Joanne and Edna, have always viewed me as a professional, a kind of support that is an essential recognition for any writer.

Christopher and Mary Pratt, and Barbara Pratt, showed me that art is both constant dedication and hard work.

I can't help but mention the unfailing enthusiasm of my sons Philip and Peter, and the cautious but well-meaning trust of my parents, Peter and Eleanor Wangersky.

As well, this collection could not have been completed without the support of Miller Ayre and the editorial staff at the *St. John's Telegram,* who both supported me and picked up the slack while I was away working on this and other writing projects.

Some versions of the stories have appeared before: "Hot Tub" was published in *Prairie Fire*, and both "Mapping" and "The Latitude of Walls" appeared in *Grain*.

ABOUT THE AUTHOR

RUSSELL WANGERSKY has received several National Newspaper Awards, won *Prism International's* Creative Non-Fiction competition two years running, won *Prairie Fire's* Creative Non-Fiction competition once, and has been a finalist for many other editorial and writing awards. His short fiction has been published in *Prairie Fire* and *Grain*. *The Hour of Bad Decisions* is his first book publication.

Born in New Haven, Connecticut, Russell Wangersky has lived in Canada since age 3, most of that time in the Maritimes. He currently works as the editor-in-chief of the *St. John's Telegram*.

MEMBER OF SCABRINI GROUP

Québec, Canada
2006